I0620029

MONTANA Fire

A Montana Romance

also by velda **BROTHERTON**

Sexy, Dark, and Gritty.

Twist of Poe Mysteries

The Purloined Skull

The Tell-Tale Stone

The Pit and the Penance

Masque of the Rising Moon

The Victorians

Wilda's Outlaw

Rowena's Hellion

Tyra's Gambler

Other Titles

Beyond The Moon

Remembrance

A Savage Grace

Once There Were Sad Songs

Stoneheart's Woman

Wolf Song

MONTANA Fire

A Montana Romance

VELDA BROTHERTON

GALWAY

OGHMA CREATIVE MEDIA

www.oghmacreative.com

Copyright © 2017 by Velda Brotherton

All rights reserved. No part of this book may be reproduced in any form without written permission from the publisher.

The characters and events in this book are fictitious. Any similarity to real persons, living or dead, is entirely coincidental and not intended by the author.

ISBN: 978-1-63373-235-3

Interior Design by Regina Hankins
Editing by Gil Miller

Galway Press
Oghma Creative Media
Bentonville, Arkansas
www.oghmacreative.com

To my Western buddy Dusty Richards

*The Montana Series came out of
your encouragement, and I'll be forever grateful.*

One

Ben hadn't been so annoyed in years as when he left Dessa's. In a fit of temper, he had agreed to do something he truly didn't want to do. He felt trapped, encircled, with no way to escape, but he would honor his word and go with her back to Kansas City. When she stepped from the train onto the platform, he would waste no time buying himself a return ticket. He had no desire to see Dessa in the company of her city friends. That would probably suit her just fine, too.

Without thought of what he was doing, Ben stomped down the street to the Busted Mule and got himself in a poker game with a couple of traveling gamblers who took every penny he had. When he returned there would be his final pay from Bannon Freight, and that was all that stood between him and abject poverty. He thought wryly that it was a good thing they refused markers at the poker table, or he'd have kept at it till he lost things he didn't have and got himself killed.

Broke and morose, he retreated to the Golden Sun, fetched Maggie literally from the arms of a man on the dance floor, and dragged her upstairs to one of the cribs. Inside, eyes flashing like cracked ice, Ben began to strip off his clothing.

Maggie sat on the edge of the bed, eyes wide. "Ben, don't.

Please, don't. You don't want to do that. Please, Ben." She just kept repeating the litany until he stood there in nothing but his underwear.

He seemed to come to himself then, his great hands fisted tightly while he stared at the woman he thought of as his sister.

"Goddammit, Maggie. Goddammit, why did she have to come here? I was doing fine, I was making it. Goddammit!"

He went to the bed, dropped to his knees, and laid his head in her lap. She smoothed his rain-soaked hair with one hand and patted at his heaving shoulders with the other.

"Oh, Ben. I'm so sorry. So sorry." She didn't know anything else to say, and so she just kept repeating herself and touching him, gentling him, until the worst had passed.

For the moment, she forgot her own distress. Samuel had laid down the law at last. Marry him or he was leaving for good, and Maggie was frightened. Love led women to situations that could be very dangerous. Men as husbands or fathers terrified her, but she loved Samuel. She hadn't decided what to do.

Later she left Ben sleeping in the bed and told Rose to tell the girls the room was taken for the evening. Rose raised her brows and Maggie said, "Ben is in there asleep." She didn't say what she was thinking. That love does terrible things to both men and women.

She did tell Rose what had happened between Ben and Dessa, or as much of it as she knew. The news distressed Rose greatly, for something terrible must have gone on between the couple, and she had no notion how to fix it.

Not yet, at any rate.

And she didn't get the chance to try, for the next morning Ben Poole and Dessa Fallon caught the stagecoach for the first leg of their trip. Rose had given Ben some money, figuring he would be too proud to let Dessa pay for personal things, even though he was technically in her employment. It would never occur to the child to pay him until they reached Kansas City. Moneyed folks didn't think about what it was like to have empty pockets.

The couple would ride down to Devil's Gate, where they would board the train headed east. Rose was terribly afraid she would never see Dessa again, and so held her an extra long time when they said their good-byes.

The storm had moved out of the mountains at daybreak and the crisp, fresh air held a tang of ice off the high peaks. In silence Ben helped Dessa aboard the stagecoach for the first leg of their long journey.

Dessa leaned from the window and looked back at Rose and Maggie, standing in the street holding their skirts up out of the mud with one hand and waving with the other until she could no longer see them. Then she settled back in the seat, not sparing even a glance for her companion, who sat across from her beside a black-frocked, bearded gentleman who had been on the stage when it pulled in to Virginia City.

The first day of October, a Saturday, found Dessa and Ben boarding the eastbound Union Pacific train, 1,014 miles from Omaha, Nebraska. Had they headed west from Omaha to Sacramento, California, the trip would take four to four and a half days, the black-frocked gentleman informed Dessa before they left the stage to board the train. She only cared how many days it was back East to Kansas City.

Their companion's name was Bugler—"like the horn," he would say each time he introduced himself. He never mentioned a given name.

He was filled with information about the infant Union Pacific Railroad, and soon his stories drove away Ben's dark scowl.

As the steam engine huffed and hooted and hissed out of

the station, Bugler related a tale that did little to relax Dessa for the long trip ahead.

"Back in January, a passenger train left Omaha headed West. Pulled by the steam engine America. She was really flying along, pushing their limits, they were. Well, sir, they soon paid for that little mistake. Weren't five miles out of Aspen, Wyoming, when all that speed done 'em in. The outside rails gave way on a curve and a coach and all three Pullmans rolled down the bank and landed upside down."

Bugler stopped. Later she would learn that he always paused at precisely the most climactic part of any story. He tamped down the tobacco in the stinking bowl of his enormous pipe.

Dessa eyed the thing and wrinkled her nose. It looked too heavy to carry around. Why would anyone want to constantly fool with something so ugly that smelled so bad?

Bugler puffed and gurgled at the pipe stem until Ben asked, "And then what happened?"

It was just what the man was waiting for, and removing the pipe from between his lips, he cleared his throat dramatically and continued the tale. "Two men were killed and more than a hundred passengers were beat up and bruised and slashed by breaking glass. A gory scene indeed."

"That's terrible," Dessa said, and stared out the window and down into a gorge. It gave her the shudders thinking about the car turning loose and rolling all the way to the bottom.

"Ah, little lady, don't you fear. That same thing would never happen again. They've already had their share of hard luck on this line. Why, it weren't two months later when the America had been back on the western run less than a week that it was derailed by a herd of cattle in western Wyoming."

Dessa was appalled. "I thought you were going to tell us it was attacked by Indians. Cattle? My goodness, one wouldn't think they could turn over a big old engine like the one pulling this car."

"Indians." Bugler snorted. "That's another tale in itself."

"Oh, don't tell me."

Obviously pleased with his attentive and easily impressed audience, Bugler launched into a long, drawn-out story of an Indian attack that had occurred on the Union Pacific run back in August of that year. "They haven't tried since, though, and folks are getting mighty complacent. Would be about right for them to hit again, when our guard is down."

Ben drew himself up and turned from the window. "Sir, you're scaring the wits out of Miss Fallon. It'd be a good idea if you could talk about something else."

Bugler snorted again and looked vaguely embarrassed. "Sorry, ma'am."

Dessa shot Ben a grateful look and he watched her for ever so long, a pensive expression on his face. She wished she knew what he was thinking. They had scarcely spoken except when it was absolutely necessary, and the trip was becoming terribly boring. Not that she wanted an Indian attack, but a little frivolity wouldn't be unwelcome. Even under the circumstances. She remembered that she had vowed to bicker with him at every turn, but could think of nothing to say.

The train ground to a halt some moments later, and Dessa's heart thumped right up in her throat. "What is it? What's happening?"

Bugler opened the side window and leaned out. "Must be thousand-mile tree. If the photographic car is here, we can get our pictures taken, though it's more popular with those who have ridden all the way from California. The tree is exactly a thousand miles from Omaha and it's become a popular place." He slid from the seat and made for the exit.

"Oh, Ben, let's get our picture made there. I'd like to take it back with me."

"If you want, it's fine with me. I've never had my picture made, and I don't reckon I ought to start now. That's for rich folks and road agents, the way I see it."

Dessa laughed. "Oh, Ben. Come. What will it hurt? Come on."

With her tugging on his arm, Ben could put up little resistance without making a spectacle of himself in front of the other passengers, who were smiling indulgently at Dessa. Some had even gotten to their feet and were making their way to the front of the car.

About that time, Bugler came back in and announced that J. B. Silvis was indeed present and would be taking stereographic photographs for anyone who wished to pose beside the thousand-mile tree. "He's from Andrew J. Russell's original group, don't you know. They photographed the Golden Spike ceremony in Promontory last year."

"Oh, Ben." She danced beside him in the aisle, tugging him along by the hand, glancing back occasionally, her eyes sparkling with excitement.

He could no longer resist, nor could he stop just the tiniest of smiles as he followed her.

"Here, let me get down first," he said when they reached the platform. "It's a big step."

She backed up against the car to let him slide past her and their bodies brushed. Electricity crackled between them and Ben paused for a moment, facing her, the tips of her breasts brushing at his chest. She wanted to reach out to him, smooth back a wind-blown lock of golden hair, but she resisted, and if he'd had anything in mind himself he let it go, too. He hopped down the steps and reached both arms up for her.

Before she took the first step, she glanced through the hazy glass of the car directly ahead of theirs. A young woman—a girl, really—glared harshly at her. When Dessa smiled, and nodded, the girl swung her face angrily away. From what Dessa could see of the coach, conditions in there were deplorable. It was crowded with roughly dressed families and hoards, of children and men who looked as if they'd not had a bath in their entire lives.

She wondered how far the young woman was going, and felt sorry for her in those crowded circumstances. Then her mind turned back to Ben and she bounced down the three steps. She had no chance to contemplate the sloping incline before Ben spanned her waist with both hands and swung her to the ground beside him. She'd never expected to be in his arms again, and she closed her eyes to keep him from seeing how she was affected by the experience. Her cheeks flamed with heat. Perhaps he would take their flush for excitement or exertion.

For a long moment, he held her against him. A pain knifed him in the heart. He would never have her, and holding her like this was just being foolish. Just the same, he couldn't let her go. He took a deep breath to quiet the rumblings of despair and finally set her feet down on the ground. Her green eyes gazed up at him, deep and somber, and he was sure he saw that same despair reflected there. Then she brushed her hands over the front of her elegant green traveling dress as if wiping away his touch, and turned from him.

She headed for the cluster of people waiting to be photographed, chewed at her lip, and tried to will away the heavy ache inside. How could she want this man so after all that had happened? He was, despite everything, the one she wanted kissing her, touching her, being with her always. She flung away the foolish thoughts. She was going home.

When it was their turn, Ben led her to stand under the

tree. He put his arm around her shoulders so whoever looked at the picture anytime in the future could see that Ben Poole had his arm around the lovely Dessa Fallon on that bright, sunny October day before she left the West and him behind to return to her life. A defiant gesture to deny the truth. They would never be together.

When the photograph had been taken, he let his arm fall from her shoulder. He felt hollow for a long time after they climbed back aboard the train. He would never get over losing her, letting her go this way.

Rose had suggested they travel first class, and Dessa, who had already traveled by rail once, readily agreed, buying her own one-way ticket and a round trip for Ben. Conditions for passengers were appalling, but greatly improved over traveling by stage-coach. Why anyone would want to travel for pleasure, Dessa had no idea. It was a necessity best gotten through with fortitude. Ben's surly disposition certainly didn't help, but she reminded herself once again that it would be best if they didn't get friendly. She turned more and more to the companionship of Mr. Bugler.

When her stomach began to rumble for lunch, Dessa remembered what she had forgotten about that maiden journey she'd made from Kansas City to Devil's Gate on her way to Virginia City. How long ago that seemed now, and how different from this trip. She had been warned about the food accommodations, but had scarcely remembered the pandemonium involved until the train pulled into a station and the conductor announced they were to take a meal at this stop.

Mr. Bugler produced one of his now familiar snorts. "Food indeed. Little better than slop. But then, one must adjust. Let's hurry off, shall we? Perhaps we can avoid some of the worst of it."

He managed to herd a puzzled Ben and a reluctant Dessa

quickly from the passenger car and into the railroad station. Elbows out to avoid crashing into milling crowds of bearded miners, disreputable individuals in ragged garments with revolvers stuck down in their belts, society matrons with gloved hands spread at their throats, and a conglomerate of those who looked much like Dessa and Ben, Bugler managed to drag them through the food line.

As Dessa followed Bugler away from the serving counter, she was bumped hard from behind and almost dropped her coffee. Some sloshed from the cup over the back of her hand, but it wasn't hot enough to burn her.

She turned and saw the girl who'd glared at her from the coach earlier. Dark hair hung in lank strands around her shoulders and it was obvious from the smell that the girl had been on the train a good long while without benefit of a wash. Her dress was threadbare and of the cheapest cotton fabric. A thick acerbic man clutched at the girl's arm.

Dessa felt so sorry for her that when the girl spat an angry epithet at her, she simply turned away. It hurt her deeply that the young woman seemed to blame her for the circumstances in which she found herself.

Ben, who had been trailing along behind Bugler and Dessa, stopped when she did, following her gaze.

"What is it? What happened?" he asked.

"Oh, nothing," Dessa murmured. "Nothing."

Ben watched the girl walk away. When he spoke, his voice sounded forlorn. "Well, come on. Let's get out of this place. It's worse than standing in a herd of wild buffalo."

"Oh, I suppose you expect me to believe you've stood in a herd of wild buffalo," Dessa said, and hurried off, having lost sight of Bugler in the crowd.

The sandwiches were soggy and the lukewarm coffee tasted

bitter. They went outside the station and leaned against the wall to eat. After a second bite into what looked suspiciously like green beef, Dessa dropped hers.

Just then the conductor leaned down from the train and shouted, "All aboard."

A small, raggedy child pounced upon Dessa's discarded sandwich and wolfed it down as his mother dragged him and carried a squalling baby toward the waiting train. Dessa followed suit, Ben right on her heels. He hoisted her up from behind and said into her ear, "You sure this trip is necessary?"

Dessa tossed her head and moved through the car back to their seats. She slid in, leaving Ben the aisle seat so she'd have the scenery beyond the window to look at during the long silences.

By the next afternoon, they'd left the mountains behind and the Great Plains rolled out ahead of them on to the horizon. Gritty air blew through the open window. The mixture of dust and punishing wind soon became unbearable, and Dessa strained at the window to close it. Ben leaned over and helped slide it shut.

"Thank you," she murmured.

"You're welcome," he said, but instead of moving over, he stiffened. "My God, look at that."

A great black cloud rose above the prairie and boiled into the sky. They watched it in awe.

"What is it? Something burning?"

"No, it's not smoke."

By that time a murmur had passed through the car from the passengers gathered at the windows on that side of the train.

"It's birds, isn't it?" one woman asked.

"Maybe," someone replied.

The cloud spread wider and higher as it approached.

"My God, my God, it's locusts," Bugler shouted. "Get the

windows closed, now. Hurry. Hurry."

He ran up and down the aisles assisting those who were having trouble sliding the panes shut. The conductor came through the car to help, and soon everyone settled back to watch the approaching cloud of insects. Without air, the car grew stifling, and several women, tightly encased in corsets and yards of heavy fabric, swooned into their seats, where concerned husbands fanned at them with white handkerchiefs.

Dessa hid a satisfied smile. She had learned from her few weeks out West that the tightly laced and hideous corset must be the first thing to go if a woman was to survive the harsh demands of such a life, and so she had dressed in a camisole, pantaloons, and a petticoat beneath the brown linen traveling frock. Uncomfortably hot, but not restricting.

The locusts struck the moving train, the enormous cloud swinging in a wide arc so that, one by one, the cars chugged right into them.

Insect bodies soon blackened the windows as they flew head-on into the iron horse, smashing themselves one upon the other until gore ran down the glass panes.

Dessa huddled further back in the corner, hands over her ears, to shut out the screams of all the women and frightened children and the sound of the hurdling insects crunching against the glass.

Ben took in the sight with amazement and the beginnings of a grin. Obviously, he was quite entertained by the entire show, inside and outside the railroad car.

"If we're not careful, they'll just pick us up and fly off with us, won't they?" he asked Bugler, who appeared casual and unconcerned.

Soon the train ground slowly to a halt, and everyone in the car grew deathly silent. Maybe they were only taking a breath before breaking loose with total hysteria. Before that could happen, the conductor shouted, "We'll be here awhile. Please remain in the car. Don't open the doors or windows."

"What is it? What's happening?" Dessa asked along with a few others.

Bugler leaned toward her. "The tracks are so slick with their slime we can't move."

The thought made her queasy, and she fought down a rising bile. Bugler nodded with a knowing look. Seasoned traveler that he was, he showed a great delight in latching on to a couple like Dessa and Ben and impressing them with his knowledge.

The conductor came through with another announcement. "It'll take a while to clear the tracks, and then we'll be on our way. As soon as the locusts clear out, we'll open the windows and get some air, but till then, please just sit tight, ladies and gentlemen. Nothing to worry about"

Dessa wished the window wasn't covered with the smashed bodies. She wanted to watch as the survivors drifted off in an undulating black swarm.

"Let me out, Ben. Maybe we can see out the back door. I want to see." She rose and shoved at his knees.

"I've never seen anyone get excited about a bunch of damned grasshoppers before," he grumbled, but slid into the aisle to let her out. "Especially dead ones," he added at her retreating back.

"Look, Ben, look." She leaned against the glass, twisting her head to see the shrinking black cloud. "They're gone," she cried, and shoved open the door to stand on the platform.

Fresh air washed over her, drying the perspiration that plastered her shirtwaist to her body. She lifted her skirts to let the wind underneath. "Oh, that feels good."

At that moment, she twirled and saw Ben watching her with

such an expression of longing that she wanted to throw her arms around him. Before she could, he glowered darkly, then turned and walked away, leaving her all alone.

Two

Just after dark, Bugler went off to heed the call of a gambler who had wandered through the car hustling up a poker game. A bit earlier, passengers had taken a second meal, no different from the first except the meat was pink rather than green and the bread was stale, not soggy. Ben had moved to the window across from Dessa when they pulled out of the last stop, and she soon lay down in her seat to sleep. Luckily the first-class car was not overcrowded like the coaches she had glimpsed while standing on the platform earlier.

For a while she couldn't sleep, but lay staring out at the glittering stars in an ebony sky. The bone-jolting starts and stops of the train made it impossible to relax, and so she was surprised when she was startled awake sometime later. Sleep had come, after all. She sat up and rubbed at her eyes, wondering what had awakened her.

"Oh, God, he's dead. He's dead. Please, no." She squinted her eyes in the direction of the pitiful cries. Ben, lay in the seat opposite her, his long legs stuck out in the aisle, his chest shuddering. She leaned toward him, touched his arm. He was wringing wet.

"I'm sorry. God forgive me, I'm sorry," he moaned.

She lay her hand on his sweat-drenched forehead. "Ben, Ben. Wake up."

He lurched upward, knocking her aside. "What? Where?" His shoulders heaved and he buried his face in both hands.

She moved to sit beside him, to touch him, to soothe him. "What is it?" she asked. "Are you all right?"

"I'm fine." A great shudder passed through him, vibrating the seat. He wiped at his face. "Sorry, didn't mean to scare you. A bad dream, that's all. Just a bad dream. Go back to sleep."

"Ben?" She touched his arm lightly.

"Leave me alone. I'm fine."

She pulled away, sat there for a long time waiting for his breathing to settle down.

After what seemed like hours of staring off into the darkness, he said, "Dessa? I'm sorry."

"About what? What are you sorry about?"

"Everything, I guess. I didn't mean it to end up this way." Regret echoed behind the words. "I thought we were going to have some fun, you and I. You're so—so carefree, and I liked that. I thought—I mean—well, hell. I didn't think it would get serious. You let me know right from the start what a buffoon you thought I was. Just an ignorant frontiersman. Now you're all puffed up and mad at me about something I don't understand, and next thing you know, I'm the one who's apologizing." He sounded far, far away.

It took her a moment to reply. "I didn't ask you to. There's no need for you to be sorry. And I did not."

He waited, too, like maybe she'd explain that last statement. When she didn't, he asked, "Did not what?"

"Did not call you an ignorant buffoon."

He sighed. "You thought it, and I am."

"I did not, and you are not." She wanted to grab him, shake him as if he were a misbehaving child. In a way, though, he was right about what she had thought at first, but no longer. "You are a sweet, gentle, and very handsome man."

"Ignorant buffoon would still fit with all that," he said in a lighter tone.

"Well, it doesn't. You're the one who... well, I mean, I was perfectly willing to—uh, what you said, have some fun, till I found you with another woman."

"I found you with that other woman, Dessa. Not the other way around."

She straightened stiffly beside him. "Well, you know exactly what I mean, Ben Poole. And her hanging on your arm all lovey-dovey and those kids treating you like their papa, or at least a long-lost and well-loved uncle. I'm not entirely innocent, you know. I understand... uh, arrangements like that."

"Arrangements? With Sarah? Oh, Dessa, my God, you don't know how wrong you are."

"Well, tell me, then. How wrong am I?"

From over the back of the seat, a voice hissed, "Would you two kindly shut up so we can get some sleep? It's the middle of the night, for God's sake."

"I second that," piped up another voice.

Ben rose and pulled her to her feet. "Come on, let's go out on the platform. It'll be cooler and I'm sure as hell not sleepy anymore."

"Well, praise be," came the voice from the other seat.

They stumbled around in the dark, making their way to the rear of the car and the platform. Once outside, he held on to her. The train rolled and rocked along, the wheels setting up a clacking rhythm that formed a steady backdrop for their conversation.

"You were about to tell me how wrong I am about you and Sarah," she said after growing accustomed to the train's movement. She was achingly aware of his proximity, the warmth of his body in the coolness of the night, his arm encircling her waist to hold her steady.

"Sarah is—Sarah *was*—"

"Are the twins yours?"

"Mine?" He laughed bitterly. "Lord, no, they're not mine. But they have no father, and I just—"

"Sarah's husband? What happened to him?"

Ben cleared his throat. This was very difficult. He'd never spoken the words aloud, the ones he needed to say to her at this very moment. He couldn't understand why it was so terribly important to him that she know about what he had done. Perhaps he was trying to drive that final wedge between them, the one that would assure she wouldn't want to be around him. Would no longer question him and care about him and play her games with him. Tell her, he commanded himself. Tell her, so she can forget forever this clumsy frontiersman she met out West. This killer.

"He died. I killed him. There, are you satisfied now? Are you happy to learn that what you thought all along was right?"

He had her by the shoulders, had her pulled up so close she could feel the warmth of his breath on her cheek. Smell him, too. This man. Oh, this wonderful man. She swayed against him.

"Oh, God, Dessa." He kissed her, a demanding kiss that frightened her with its intensity. A moan escaped his throat, vibrating over her tongue as she opened her lips to him. He released the tight grip on her arms and encircled her in an embrace that was anything but fierce. He cradled her lovingly, head bent down to taste her mouth, her eyes, her throat.

She collapsed into that caress, the flavor and texture of him encompassing her entire world. Where he touched her she was on fire, she yearned for more as he tongued the hollow of her throat. A sound like crying spiraled from deep within her. He lowered his head, nibbled at her breast through the thickness of fabric.

"Oh, Ben." She grasped his head, holding him there, begging for more as shards of pleasure burst through her to tingle every nerve ending.

The little nuzzling sounds he made were of pure content, pure desire, animalistic and unreal. The heat of his breath flowed through the material and over her breast, and she wanted to bare herself to him. Rip the dress away and feel his warm, moist lips fastened around each nipple in turn. Feed him, nurture him, hold him always and forever, while he awoke in her the fiercest passion she had ever experienced. Would ever experience.

She panted with the exertion, backed into the corner against the rail and the rear of the car. He fell to his knees, buried his face in the heavy folds of her dress so that the pounding of his hot, ragged breath filtered through to the flesh between her legs. She clung to him, with him, around him, as if he were inside her. The swaying of the train set up a rhythm and they moved with it.

He groaned and grabbed her buttocks in both hands.

She threw her head back and cried out to a black universe that rotated until she grew dizzy. She crumpled, and he caught her up close, nibbling and licking at her neck, repeating her name over and over.

Head on his shoulder, she gasped and tried to recapture some feeling of equilibrium. What had he done to her? How could this have happened? She had never heard of such a thing. Mother never talked to her about this.

"Ben, what..?"

He touched her cheek with the back of his hand. "Are you all right?"

She nodded, struck mute by the enormity of what had happened.

"Are you sure?" he asked, and brushed hair away from her face. "Here, let me help you up."

She felt wobbly, strange, as if just recovering from a long illness. "Not yet. Just a minute."

"I'm sorry, Dessa."

"No," she gasped. "No, don't you dare tell me you're sorry for... for this." She brushed her bodice, then his chest. "For what we've done. Don't you be sorry. I will not allow you to be sorry anymore, not for anything."

Ben untangled himself and rose, left her kneeling there. God, what had he done? He had wanted her, suddenly and so fiercely that he couldn't help himself. But she hadn't tried to stop him, had she? If she had, would he have been able to stop? How could he feel such desire for a woman like her? It was as if she had bewitched him with her city ways, and no matter what he did, he couldn't fight her magnetism.

He might as well have torn her clothes from her body and had his way with her, considering her response. Dear God, they had both experienced a release of their pent-up desires; their passion for each other had been spent without the act itself being completed. He had never known such a thing could happen.

He wanted to explain it to her, somehow make things the way they were. How would they ever bear to part, feeling this way about each other? Or perhaps this wasn't love, but simply an animal attraction that would go away once they weren't in each other's sight any longer.

She collected herself and used the railing to stand. Without speaking further, he guided her back inside and to her seat. A metallic gleam lightened the eastern sky, warning of impending sunrise and another long day of traveling. He settled down beside her and pulled her head onto his shoulder.

She turned and nestled comfortably into the curve of his arm. She didn't think of his earlier confession until much later, after she had recovered somewhat from the incident on the platform.

He said he had killed Sarah's husband. How could that be? How could this gentle, beautiful man ever have killed anyone? There had to be an explanation. She pushed the memory to the back of her mind. She would not ask him any more about it, didn't want to know.

Oddly, she dreamed of Mitchell, and even more strange, he stood just out of her sight, beckoning from a thick and dark grove of trees. In the dream she could not recognize the place where they were, but she knew her brother, and he looked just as he had the day he rode away to war, waving his white hat high in the air until that was all she and Mother and Father could see—that hat gleaming in the ferocious sunlight.

Then a monster came to chase Mitchell away, to turn on her, and she saw that it was the vicious outlaw Coody

She awoke with tears on her cheeks and her brother's name on her lips, but before she could talk about the dream, it had flown from her memory just like the dust blew across this endless prairie.

The day dragged on interminably, broken only by infrequent stops along the way and the sawdust taste of the awful food and brackish water.

The train had just pulled out after lunch when the door to the car burst open with such force that the resulting crack of it hitting the seats against the wood-paneled wall brought exclamations from everyone in the car.

"Robbery! It's a robbery." The words echoed from one to the other of the passengers. A tremendous man entirely filled the doorway. Legs spraddled, he held one arm cocked just above the butt of a huge pistol tucked in his belt. He wore a high-crowned black hat, a strange kind of leather britches fastened on over dusty black pants, a faded shirt, and a black-and-gray-striped vest. A limp bandanna was tied around his neck.

Immediately Dessa thought of Coody and the stage robbery, and grabbed Ben's arm so tightly he grunted.

"Lookee here at the swells," the man crowed. "Well, let's just see how you like this." He yanked the tremendous revolver out of his waistband and fired it off, aiming toward the ceiling of the car. The bullet punched a hole through the roof.

Ladies screamed and men shouted. The man laughed uproariously, fired the pistol a couple more times, laughing all the harder at the reaction. Women cringed and hid behind their men, who in turn blustered but did nothing to stop the wild man's antics.

Ben, who carried no weapon, put himself between the man and Dessa, a stalwart barrier of protection.

The conductor entered through the other end of the car just as the desperado backed out, slammed the door, and was gone.

Instead of going after the man, the calm railway employee made his way slowly up the aisle, soothing the passengers' fears and making sure no one was injured.

One exclaimed so that Dessa and Ben could hear, "Hurt? I could have had apoplexy. What is the meaning of such a thing? An attempted robbery, sir, and you not doing a whit about it. I'll report this to the president of the Union Pacific as soon as we reach our destination."

The conductor said, "He was just blowing off steam, sir. I assure you, this train has never been robbed. The cowpunchers, well, sir, they just have to blow sometimes. Some of 'em are riding back after a long and harsh trail drive pushing cattle north. It gets crowded and hot in the coaches and they will bring whiskey along—well, you understand."

He addressed the speech to everyone. Their murmurs and exclamations were quieting down now that the danger, if there had ever been any, was past.

"Damned fool," Ben grumbled. "Suppose someone on the car had a gun. Could have shot him. Damned fool."

"Happens a lot," Bugler said. He'd returned bleary-eyed and morose from his long stint at the poker table, and these were the first words he'd spoken since lowering himself with a groan into the seat an hour or so earlier. "Got robbed myself and no one ever drew a gun. I tell you, every time one of those card-sharps plies their trade on me, I swear I'll never do it again. But along one comes, and despite everything, I trot right on his heels and give him all my money.

"Took 'em a mite longer to break me this time, though. I reckon I'm learning their ways some."

With that statement, Bugler dropped his cold pipe down in the pocket of his jacket, leaned his head back, and went to sleep.

As the afternoon wore on, dust grew thicker until the windows had to be closed to prevent everyone choking. Dessa fussed with long strands of her dark hair that had come loose from the pins. Her black hat, the one she'd worn to the funeral and which seemed the best suited to travel with the veil turned back, had long since been removed in the hopes she would be cooler without it. Nothing seemed to help. Opening the windows was unthinkable.

Ben unbuttoned his shirt halfway down. "Loosen your dress at the neck. It'll help," he said.

She nodded, but glanced around to see if anyone was watching.

"Don't worry about any of them. They've all got their own troubles," he said, and began to undo her buttons. His big fingers were clumsy and fumbled with the small loops.

Dessa smiled at the furrow of concentration between his eyes, the firm set of his mouth, and gently grazed her fingertips over his cheek. Dear Ben. How could she have ever thought him bumbling and ignorant?

He stopped, his hands grazing her hot skin, and tilted his head so that his lips touched her fingers.

At that very moment, the train lurched and emitted a hideous squealing sound. It jolted to a stop, and on down the line behind them car after car thudded into the one ahead of it. With each hit the car they were in leaped forward again, then it would groan to a stop. On and on this went, until Dessa thought her insides would be bounced out.

Once the train stopped moving and making the hideous screeching noise, everyone gathered at their windows to peer out.

Below, Dessa saw no land, just the yawing space of a deep gorge. At the bottom a miniature stream flowed, rocks and trees jutted out of a bluff far off in the distance.

"It's a trestle. We're on a trestle," Ben said, looking out the window next to her.

"Fire, fire," came the shout down the line as doors were flung open. "The bridge is on fire. A brigade, we need a fire brigade."

Ben left his seat. Bugler, roused by all the commotion, joined him. Dessa remained by the window, peering first toward the front of the train, which she couldn't see because it curved away out of sight, then to the back, which she could see. Thick, black smoke billowed into the sky where the wind tossed it away.

She leaped from her seat and ran in the direction Ben had gone.

"Please, ladies, keep your seats," the conductor urged as he hurried through the car. He stopped until Dessa took a seat, then went on. She sprang up as soon as he left the car.

Ben, where was Ben? Gathered on the platform were several men, sleeves rolled up. One by one they stepped down off the train and disappeared from her view. She hurried through the door in time to see the last man swing out of sight.

"What's happened? What is it?" a young woman from the coach ahead cried. She poked her head out the door, eyes huge, her face pale with fright. Dessa saw that it was the girl who had sworn at her earlier.

Ignoring her, Dessa leaned over the rail to see better. The men were inching along a narrow walkway alongside the tracks. Once again she glanced down into the abyss and gasped with horror. Just looking down made her dizzy. She had never liked heights. As a child she couldn't even climb trees or look out a second-story window. If any one of those men fell, he would be dashed to pieces on the jagged rocks in the stream below.

She imagined the bodies spiraling ever downward, and leaned back, holding a hand over her mouth. The thick oily smell of smoke and the depth of the gorge turned her stomach.

The girl said right at her elbow, "The train set the bridge on fire. The engine set the bridge on fire. That's what the man said. Isn't that a crazy thing? Who ever heard of such a thing? And where will they get water to put it out? I ask. Perhaps they can just piss on it, all of those men, and it will go out. That's probably what they all think, isn't it, now? Men would." She chuckled harshly.

Dessa was shocked at such language from the mouth of a lady, but before she could voice her opinion, the girl was off on another tack.

"I told Keenan, I says, this place is a crazy place. Bad enough to come to America, but then on top of it to traipse all over these plains. What are we looking for? is what I'm asking. Now, if he gets killed out there, falls off and smashes himself on the rocks below, what will I do then? I ask you, what will I do?"

How odd that the young woman spoke as if she'd never been angry with Dessa. She had a thick accent that made her hard to understand, but she seemed to speak English without much trouble.

Dessa tried to reassure her. "He won't, I'm sure. The railroad certainly wouldn't let its passengers risk their lives, would they?"

"Well, now, listen to you," the girl sneered. "And ain't you miss prim and proper? Riding in the ritzy car while us that has naught is hauled along like herds of swine. You think them rich bastids care about the likes of us... or even you, for that matter?"

Shocked into silence, Dessa ignored the girl and leaned out very cautiously, trying to spot Ben. Toward the rear of the train she saw a platform protruding out from the bridge, and on it a huge barrel. A bucket brigade had been formed from the barrel, which obviously held water, and the men from the train, who had lined up to the place from which the black smoke boiled, were passing the buckets along.

Balanced precariously as they were on the narrow walkway, passing water to the fire was a slow and tedious job. She wished she could pick out Ben in the line, but with the smoke and her eyes already blurred from so much dust and sweat, and being afraid to lean out any farther, she couldn't.

The girl who had rattled on in her strangely accented voice lifted her skirts and climbed up to sit on the hand rail.

Dessa reached toward her, cried out a warning, and the train shuddered. The girl lost her hold, teetered, and tumbled backward.

She screamed but managed to grab the rail with one hand. There she hung, legs kicking about and one arm swinging out in space. Her slight body twisted and turned. Her legs weren't long enough to put her feet down on the narrow walkway. Nor could she turn loose and drop, for she would surely lose her balance and her footing and fall from the bridge into the chasm below. She screamed again, a terrified, high-pitched wail that rent the air, overpowering the shouts of the men fighting the fire.

Dessa leaned out and grabbed the girl's wrist, as slick with sweat as were her own hands.

Oh, God, she couldn't hold on.

The girl raised frantic eyes, her loose arm clawing toward Dessa. No sound came from her open mouth. Horror had stricken her dumb.

Swallowing a great lump that rose from deep in her gut, Dessa shouted, "Hang on, hang on. I'll get you."

She peered over the side, closed her eyes, and swayed. Oh, dear God, she couldn't do it. She would fall! They both would fall.

She stepped down off the platform to the wooden step. A great chasm yawned in front of her. Turning her back, she reached blindly with one foot for the next step, and then the next. Her stomach quivered, and for a moment she froze in place. While the girl dangled by one fragile arm, Dessa finally found her footing on the very narrow wooden walkway of the bridge.

"Don't look down, don't look up, just don't look," she muttered. Hanging on tightly with one hand, she stretched the other toward the girl. The sound of her shoe soles sliding along the walkway grated in her ears, and stars shot through her vision. She was going to pass out!

A strange hideous gurgle came from the girl. "I can't... I can't hold on."

Dessa took a deep breath, gritted her teeth, and peered through the burning perspiration. The girl's wide-eyed glance locked on her. Pleading, begging. Don't let me fall. Don't.

Her outstretched hand still wouldn't reach the girl. Hanging on to the narrow rail posts with first one hand, then another, she inched closer. She did not look anywhere but into the terrified face watching her progress. Under the balls of her feet, the walkway offered safety, the rails gave a hold, and she just kept moving. Don't think of what's below. Don't…think.

The girl dragged in a great gasp. "Me fingers is slipping offffff."

"No, no," Dessa cried. Grabbing at the rail with her right hand, she flung her left around the girl's waist just as the girl's fingers slipped away from their flimsy hold on the rail.

The girl kicked and screamed and fought.

"Stop, stop it," Dessa shouted at her. "We'll both fall. I've got you, I've got you."

Muscles across her shoulders strained as she held up the girl's weight and most of her own with the grip of that right hand. "Put your feet on the walk."

Instead, panicked, the girl threw a frail arm around Dessa's neck and kicked and pumped her legs, trying to climb up her body. Gasping, Dessa clawed for the rail, got a firm hold, and there they both hung. The arms clamped around her throat were cutting off her air. She gasped and tried to move back toward the steps, but she couldn't do it.

They were both going to fall. They would die.

Her vision blackened, but she hung on tightly, inhaling the sour smell of fear from the unwashed body clinging to her. She clamped her jaws and struggled to pull them both along to the steps, such a sparse few feet away. They weren't going to make it. She simply couldn't pull the weight of both of them, not with the girl hanging on her like that. Dangling out over the precipice.

The girl was crying uncontrollably, making huge wet sounds down in her throat.

The fingers of Dessa's right hand slipped ever so slightly on the rail and she gasped for air.

Abruptly an arm clamped around her, a voice said sternly, "I've got you, stop fighting."

"Ben, oh, Ben."

"Turn loose, little one, we've got you," another male voice said, and the weight of the girl was released from around her neck.

Dessa dragged in a deep lungful of air, still clinging to the rail, even though Ben had a good hold on her.

As she was pulled away, the girl pawed out at Dessa, as if afraid to let her go. Then the other man had her. With one hefty sweep, Ben swung Dessa onto the bottom step of the platform.

Trembling so hard she couldn't speak, she latched on to the rail on either side and hung there, dragging sweet air into her aching lungs. Ben spanned her body from behind, his own hands closing over hers, and let her rest against him until she could climb the steps back to safety.

"What in God's name were you thinking of?" he said when he had her safely in his arms.

"She fell... she fell, and I couldn't... I couldn't let her... oh, Ben. I was so frightened. I couldn't see or hear. My voice wouldn't work. I have never felt anything like that in my entire life. I'm afraid...I've always been afraid of being up high and falling."

"Well, you didn't fall. And let's hope you don't ever try anything like that again."

Abruptly her knees turned to rubber and he swept her up

in his arms, his mouth crooking into that familiar grin she hadn't seen in a while.

"Guess this is just becoming a habit we can't break," he said, and carried her inside to their seat.

Three

Bugler, revived after the excitement of the bridge fire, filled them in on the history of the span that had almost taken Dessa's life.

"It's called Dale Creek Bridge."

"Creek?" Dessa said. "That's more than a creek."

"Yes, well, these railroad folk are prone to massive understatement quite frequently. At any rate, it's an engineering marvel. A timber trestle 560 feet long and 130 feet above that tiny stream. Everyone said it would fall under the first freight."

"Oh, great. Good. Not only do we set it on fire, we could have made it collapse under us simply by being there." Dessa shuddered at the recollection of dangling out over that sheer drop and tried to forget the heart-rending terror of it. "What set it on fire, by the way?"

"Sparks from the engine. That's why they keep buckets of water on those platforms. You'll see them on all these wooden trestles."

"You mean we may have to do that again?"

Ben laughed and hugged her close. "Well, not the part where you try to take a dive off the train, let's hope. No, we don't have to do that again."

The two men chuckled, but Dessa's attempt died in her throat. It really wasn't very funny to her. In her mind's eye she could still see her fingers slipping off that rail, and her and that irascible and hysterical young woman tumbling into the chasm of Dale Creek. The memory was too raw, too frightening.

Ben sensed her trembling, held her closer, and put his lips in her hair. "That was a very brave thing to do."

"I didn't think about it being brave. I just did it because of her eyes, the terror there. And me doing nothing might have been the last thing she saw as she fell. I knew if I didn't do something, I'd be seeing that face filled with terror for the rest of my life."

Ben knew exactly what she meant. He would carry forever the haunting memory of Clete Woodridge lying in his own blood in the dusty street, death already masking his features as he looked up at Ben, begged, "Take care of Sarah. And the boys, take care of my boys."

Ben shook away the memory. Clete hadn't known that Ben's bullet had killed him, but Ben knew, and so he'd promised. Rose kept telling him he was foolish, that sooner or later he had to live his own life and Sarah had to live hers. But he couldn't let go, he just couldn't. Not without seeing Clete's accusing stare for the rest of his days.

Right at this moment, though, none of that mattered nearly as much as the girl he held in his arms, and he gave her an extra big hug. He might live with losing her, but he couldn't bear to think of her dying.

She grunted and giggled. "You'll choke me if you keep that up. I'm okay, thanks to you. You weren't exactly a coward yourself. If it weren't for you, she and I would both have been smashed in the bottom of that rocky ravine."

He inhaled deeply of her scent. When he'd heard the screams and saw her dangling out in space, he realized that he loved her more than life itself. He would have plunged to his death to save her, and it was a knowing that planted itself firmly within his heart and soul. He might never have her for his own, they would certainly have to part at the end of this journey, but he would carry that love for the rest of his life. And he knew, too, how very rare and privileged such a thing was. To love, to be loved. Could one outweigh the other? He didn't think so. And one didn't hinge on the other, either.

"Oh, Dessa, Dessa, I love you," he said in her ear.

Swallowing over the lump in her throat, she leaned back into his embrace. What would they do? Her on her way to take over the reins of her daddy's business in a city Ben would hate on sight, and Ben set to return to Sarah and her boys, whatever reasons he had for that relationship.

Why couldn't this trip last forever, miserable as it was? Then she could remain in his arms and never face the parting that must surely come.

She turned so that her lips brushed his jaw. "I love you, too, Ben Poole. I love you, too."

The sweet declaration was a balm for his battered soul. He refused to think of their parting.

Sometime later that afternoon, when everyone in the car appeared to be dozing, Dessa was startled by a tug on her sleeve. She opened her eyes to see the dirty face of the young woman who'd almost pulled them both to their deaths.

Dessa rubbed her hands over her eyes, thinking for a moment she was dreaming. "What? What is it?"

"Me man says I should ask you."

Dessa nodded and waited. What could she say?

The girl picked at a patch on her soiled skirt. "I said no, and he got mad at me. Hollered was I a heathen or what? And I 'spect that's what I am, for sure." She fingered the rich cloth of Dessa's dress.

"Surely to goodness will never have a dress as fine as that, and your skin. Lookit." Roughly she grabbed Dessa's hand and rubbed her calloused thumb over its back. The pad was so coarse it scratched Dessa.

Dessa pulled away. "What do you want?" Deep down inside, she was frightened of this little waif with the angry eyes and bad breath.

"You saved me hide, and I thought as how you'd seen fit to do that, you might... well, you just might give me and me man something. We tried to homestead some land, but nothing worked out for us and we near starved. Finally just give up while we still had the fare to come back East. Well?" Her filmy eyes fixed on Dessa.

"You want money?" She couldn't believe what she had heard. "You want me to give you money because I saved your...your life? That doesn't make sense."

The girl dropped her gaze. "I told him it wouldn't work. Rich folks don't ever see fit to share nothing, that's how they stay rich."

"Your husb...your man put you up to this?"

The poor waif nodded. At least she had the good sense to look ashamed of her part in the scheme. "I'm sorry. Oh, God, I was so scared when I pitched over the side. I seen me flat as a pancake down on them rocks. I do truly thank you, and I'll tell me man you said no." She slanted a quick look up through her eyelashes. "I reckon he'll smash me about some, but that's okay. I ain't dead on the rocks, now, am I? Thanks to you."

She rose from her squatting position in the aisle and started to walk away. Dessa grabbed her arm.

"Wait, don't go. Here." She dug around in her reticule. Most of her trip money was secreted on her person, not easily retrieved in public, but she did carry a small roll of bills for emergency expenses. She slipped it into the girl's hand and held on to her for a minute.

The idea that this child/woman would get beaten if she didn't return to her man with money outraged Dessa. She wanted to follow her into the other car and tell her man so, but that would probably only cause more trouble.

The girl didn't look at the wad of money, but searched Dessa's eyes beseechingly. "I'd get away from him if there was another way. But me pap promised me to him, and the money he paid fed me brothers and sisters. Tisn't so bad, really."

She stumbled away, not looking back or uttering a word of thanks. For a long time after the door had closed behind the girl, Dessa stared through the glass. How poor was the girl's existence, how luxurious her own. It amazed her how her life could be so richly blessed without her ever realizing it. The incident stuck with her a long while as she sat in silence, watching Ben sleep and listening to the monotonous clacking of the train wheels carrying her home.

Exhausted and dirty, Ben and Dessa at last detrained at Kearney, Nebraska, to catch another train south to Kansas City. She was almost home.

Standing in the station, luggage around her feet, her trunk left on the platform for transfer for the last leg of the trip, she was filled with a mixture of pleasure and dread. By this time tomorrow, Ben would be on his way back west; out of her life forever. She would never see him again.

Eyes filling with unexpected tears, she turned to him. "Ben, let's stay over a day here. We can get hotel accommodations, take a bath, eat some decent food. I'm not sure I can go on in such a condition." She held her arms away from her body and made a face, as if a bath were her only real concern.

She wanted simply to ask him to stay with her. Forget everything and stay with her when they reached her destination. But she couldn't. He would be miserable, and in time so would she. And suppose he refused? Suppose he turned his back on her and left anyway? That would simply kill her. Better to part knowing they loved each other. That if things had been different, they could have been happy. A mutually agreed-upon parting would be bittersweet, and it would remain forever in her memory, untouched by time or aging or strife. In a dime novel, the whole thing would be so romantic. But in true life, the hopelessness of the situation caused a terrible ache around her heart.

Ben touched the tip of her chin and stared down into her brimming eyes. He almost asked her at that moment to come with him. Together, they could climb on that train headed west and just ride until there was no place else to ride. Nothing but the ocean stretching to the horizon. He'd never seen the ocean, couldn't even imagine what it might be like to behold that great expanse of water flowing to meet the sky. He pictured Dessa at his side, took in a great gasp of air.

His voice trembled when he asked, "Won't he be looking for you?"

"He?" she asked.

"Arthur or Andrew, or whatever his name is."

"I can telegraph, say I'll be delayed."

He took her hand, held it to his lips for an instant. "Are you sure this is what you want?" One more night with her, one more night. Would that make their parting easier? The answer, of course, was no, but nevertheless he wanted this time.

She nodded solemnly, wondering exactly what she was agreeing to. Would she let him make love to her? The very idea made her dizzy. If she did such a thing and then he went away, no man would ever have her. She would have only two choices then: become a spinster or a loose woman to be whispered about all over town. Was that what she wanted?

"I only want a bath and a decent bed. That's all I want," she said aloud.

"Yes, of course," he murmured against her skin, and turned her hand loose.

And so she wired Andrew a terse message, and they checked in to a hotel near the Union Station, requesting separate rooms and hot baths. Ben paid for his own from the money Rose had loaned him. No telling when he could pay her back, but he would. He had no intention of taking money from Dessa for traveling to Kansas City with her. Once he got to California and settled down, he would find work. He'd heard that out there jobs were plentiful and the pay was good.

Ben carried his own bag and hers, and she followed along upstairs to their rooms. They arranged to meet for supper after they had bathed.

Even in the small restaurant of the hotel, Ben felt uncomfortable. It wasn't at all like Virginia City. They were "back East." They were in the United States. Men and women both dressed differently and spoke differently. Hell, they even walked strange. Seated at the small table across from Dessa, he found himself not knowing where to put his elbows. First he planted them on both sides of his dinner service; then, because that took up too much of the sorry little table, he tucked them down against his sides stiffly, and that made it difficult to eat.

What exactly was that green stuff on his plate, anyway? He poked at it with his fork, decided it was some kind of weed blossom, and shoved it aside to tackle the rest of the meal.

The tiny chunk of beef did look safe to eat, but there weren't over two or three bites. It was covered with a strange puddinglike sauce that he dipped a tine of his fork in and tasted cautiously. Definitely not gravy, but spicy. It would do, especially since he was hungry enough to eat a horse. He felt much like the frontier buffoon Dessa had thought him, and he couldn't wait to get out of this place. He wouldn't stay in Kansas City, either, for it was bound to be even worse. Ben Poole faced the fact that the States were not for him. He was a frontiersman, no doubt about it.

Dessa enjoyed the first decent meal she had eaten since leaving Kansas City to go to the territories. Looking around her, she sighed, then glanced at Ben, who managed to look quite distressed, though he was eating his meal with gusto.

She sipped from her glass of water, cleared her throat, plucked her napkin from her lap and patted her mouth. His discomforting scowl made her uneasy.

"What is it, Ben?" she asked in a half whisper.

His hand jerked, spilling food from the fork on its way to his mouth. "Hell if I know. Eat it anyway, it's probably good for you."

Dessa couldn't help chuckling. "I didn't mean that, silly. I meant, what's wrong? You look like you swallowed a thundercloud."

He put the fork carefully in his plate. "They're dressed funny and this stuff tastes awful," he said, leaning toward her so that he could keep his voice low. "It's worse than the Continental in Virginia, but at least there folks don't put on such a show. Look at 'em, Dessa."

She did. The women wore crinolines so that their skirts billowed out around them to fill the aisles between the tables. The men were in frock coats with cravats at the throats of their boiled white shirts. She herself had owned one of the new bustles before leaving for Virginia City, and thought them much more comfortable than the crinolines. But if she were to admit the truth, she would agree with Ben. Folks on the frontier knew much more about dressing for comfort than the people here.

"Well, Ben, how you dress doesn't mean anything."

Ben guffawed and heads turned. "Would if I had to wear that getup," he said, and gestured toward a man nearby who had a bow tie up under double chins, the turned-over collar of his shirt buttoned so tight he was red in the face.

"Well, Ben, what I meant was that you look just fine."

He touched the rough fabric of his sack coat. "Wasn't talking about me," he grumbled.

If Ben thought these people were turned out fancy, wait until he… But then it didn't really matter, did it? He wouldn't be attending the welcome-home party that was sure to be thrown when her friends learned she was back. By then he would be on the train headed for Montana Territory, and no longer caring about what she did or who she did it with.

She looked up in time to see Ben toss his napkin in the middle of his plate and rise. "I'm just going out for a walk, Dessa, if that's all right with you."

She stood also. "You don't need my permission, but I think I'll just go back to my room and go to bed."

He nodded and threaded his way carefully between the seated couples, taking great care to keep his boots off the women's billowing spotted and striped skirts.

She felt a sense of intense sorrow and loss when he left the table. He was as much out of place here as if he had stumbled into a church in only his underdrawers. Funny how easily she had fitted in out in Montana. She had to admit that she had hoped Ben would develop an instant attraction to the way of doing things here. But it had been a dim hope and one she really hadn't expected would come true.

After she went alone to her room, it was a long time before she fell asleep, despite her exhaustion. She kept thinking of what the next few days would bring. How would she sort out the affairs of her daddy's business when she knew nothing about it? Should she sell it or try to find someone to run it? What would she tell Andrew when he asked her once again to marry him? When would Ben come back to the hotel? Had he gone to seek the company of a fancy woman?

That last thought filled her with a longing for his embrace. She thought of the passion he had awakened in her and her body felt hot with desire. His breath against her throat, his lips at her breast, teeth finding her nipples even through the layers of her clothing.

Dessa moaned and pulled her knees up tightly against her chest. "Ben, oh, Ben."

A long shaft of golden light cut the darkness of the street. Ben headed for it, stomping hard on the wooden boardwalk to get rid of the unexpected anger that rode within him. Why was he so angry? And who was he angry with?

Drawing up to the batwing doors, he peered inside, pretending that he was just taking a look, when all along he knew he would go in. It would be a toss-up between a couple of beers or a hand or two of poker. Maybe both. Hell, who cared?

The place was pretty tame compared to the Busted Mule or even Rose's place. But in the far corner a card game was in progress, and so he carried his mug of beer over and stood to watch.

"Well, Doc, you in or what?" the dealer asked of a white-haired gentleman who wore a watch fob and a golden chain across his vested and quite large midsection.

"I'm thinking."

"Well, don't take the whole night to do it," said a young, rough-looking man sitting near Ben.

Ben glanced at the hand and saw three treys and two jacks.

"What's the bet?" Doc asked, his fingers playing over a stack of blue chips.

"Hunnerd. Bet or pass, old man," the young tough said.

Ben coughed and gulped at his beer, hoping the older man would just fold and walk away. He'd never beat a full house.

Doc looked all around and laid down his cards. "Reckon I'm out."

Ben let out a breath and watched the next man.

He looked to be a farmer, with protruding ears and a sunburn across the bridge of his nose. He held his pants up with suspenders and there was a patch on the sleeve of his faded shirt. Ben shook his head at him, and the farmer studied his cards some more, looking back at Ben before laying them down.

"Me, too."

The young one shot Ben a dark look. "Step back from me when I'm playing cards, mister," he said, and raked in the pot.

Ben was in no mood to be messed with. He was about to lose the woman he loved to a way of life he purely didn't understand, and that was making him angry in a way he only vaguely remembered being angry. That was back in the war when he realized that every man in his patrol was dead but him. Then he hadn't been sure if the anger was because he was still alive or because they were all dead. And the hot fury had been so mixed up with grief that he wasn't sure he could tell the two apart.

Whatever the feeling was, he didn't like it, and so most of the time he worked it off with physical labor of some sort.

This time he couldn't.

The young tough half rose and said, "Hear what I said, mister? Move away—now."

Ben shoved the fellow back down in his chair. And he did it out of pure orneriness. And he didn't care. He was going to lose Dessa and someone had to pay.

It was just a little shove, nothing violent, Ben thought later. It sure did set the fellow off, though. He came up out of that chair like a bobcat fighting for his female, lighting all over Ben, who was easily twice his size. He latched on to Ben around the neck, locking both legs around his thighs.

"Well, hell." Ben plucked the man off, tossing him halfway across the room.

The tough rolled like a wooden barrel, fetching up against the bar while folks moved aside, holding their mugs high and out of the way.

"Sic him, you little fart," an old drunk at one of the tables shouted. "Don't you let that big old feller throw you around thataway."

Ben shrugged and turned his back on his opponent. That was the wrong thing to do, he realized shortly, for this time he was locked in a leg hug that did little damage, but made it impossible for him to walk away.

He thunked his opponent smartly on top of the head, just enough to get him to turn loose, and the fellow bit him right through his britches. Ben let out a howl and dragged his attacker off by the hair.

As fights go, it wasn't much of one. The little man never got enough of a distance from Ben for him to haul off and bust him one. It was more of a wrestling match than anything, with Ben afraid to get too rough for fear he'd kill the little son of a bitch. On the other hand, he was bitten, gouged, butted, kicked, and scratched before he finally picked the man up and toted him outside, and threw him in the water trough next to the hitching post.

"Stay in there, or I'll drown you," he commanded, holding the sputtering fool by his shirt collar. "You hear me? Don't come out of there till I'm out of sight. I mean it, now. You wrap yourself around me one more time and I'll break your arm."

The old drunk had followed the action out to the street and stood swaying around on the edge of the walk. He continued to egg the man in the horse trough on to finer deeds.

"Silly little bastid, if you'd a just listened to me, you'd a had him whupped. Now look at yah. Look like a blamed skinny wet chicken. Come out a there, I'll finish the job fer him." The drunk danced around awhile, rotating his doubled fists in the direction of the unfortunate man in the water trough.

Ben felt like throwing the old codger in, too, but he restrained himself. One battle a night was enough, and besides, he didn't feel angry anymore. All he felt was just plain tired.

He headed back toward the hotel, fingering his swollen lip gingerly. The man had brought blood with his teeth and fingernails. All things considered, he was quite a little scrapper, but he had learned the fallacy of that old adage, "The bigger they are, the harder they fall."

Ben couldn't help chuckling when he thought of how the fight must have looked to spectators. That little runt just coming back over and over, time after time being tossed clean across the room. And when you got right down to it, Ben was at fault. You didn't go standing behind a man in a poker game and giving away his hand to the other players. Anybody'd done that to him, he'd have cleaned his plow, and quick.

Come to think of it, Ben thought with another chuckle, that's what the poor little fool had tried to do. He just hadn't been quite big enough.

He tried to make no noise letting himself into his hotel room, but the bed creaked and moaned when he lowered his tired body onto the mattress. After sleeping on a bedroll on the ground most of his life, Ben had trouble relaxing on something so soft, and so he tossed and turned and the bed chirped and squawked.

The noise awoke Dessa from a light sleep, and after listening awhile, she got up and went to the door between the two rooms. She twisted the knob and found Ben hadn't locked his side, so she slipped through and into his room.

Her heart pounded fiercely. It was a wonder Ben didn't hear the drumming as she padded on bare feet across the cool wooden floor. He turned over once again; the bed groaned.

In a sliver of moonlight she could barely see the huge lump he made.

Suddenly, without warning, he sat straight up in bed and let out a few grumbled curses. The movement startled Dessa and she screeched.

That awoke Ben, who'd been dreaming the fight over again, and he hollered, "What the hell?"

"Ben, it's me. Dessa. Are you ill?"

"Ill? No, of course not. You gave me a hell of a fright. What's the matter with you, woman? Sneaking up on me like that. If I'd a had a gun, I'd a shot you. Are you okay? Is something wrong?"

She was quiet for a moment, considering whether she should just leave. He made the decision for her by fumbling around on the bedside table, finding a sulfur match, and lighting the lamp.

"Ben, what happened to your face?"

He touched the swollen lip, feeling a little ashamed.

"Did you get in a fight?" She went to his side, sat on the edge of the mattress, and studied the injuries up close. "And your eye." She touched the raw skin with the tips of her fingers.

Ben licked at the cut on his lip and grimaced.

"Oh, Ben, what happened?"

He lifted his shoulders and didn't answer right away. How could he tell her what had happened? It sounded so blamed dumb.

"Nothing much. Just a little scuffle is all."

"Why, Ben Poole. I never thought I'd see you get in a fight."

"Just shows what you know about me, Dessa Fallon. I've had plenty of fights, I reckon."

"Oh, yeah. Just how many fights have you had?" She was teasing him now, and feeling very exposed, sitting on the edge of his bed in her nightdress, and him bared to the waist and only wearing his long johns.

Without thinking, she leaned closer and gently kissed the swollen lip. Ben closed his eyes and sighed. She kissed the corner of his puffy red eye.

"Oh, Ben. Please, Ben. I don't know if I can... I mean, how can we—"

She didn't get the rest said. He wrapped his arms around her, gathered her close, and laid his head in the hollow of her shoulder. He smelled of the soap he had bathed in, and his freshly washed hair tickled her chin.

"I knew this would happen. I just knew it would," he said, his breath hot against her throat. "I can't stay here, Dessa. I plain just can't. And you have to. I see that. Dammit, why did this happen? Why couldn't we have just gone on our separate ways? Say you'll come back to Montana with me. Now, Dessa.

Now. Or just leave me be. Don't come near me like this, tempting me with every breath."

He pulled back, taking her by the shoulders so he could look into her eyes. She saw twin flames burning there from the lamplight, saw his suffering, too.

When she closed her eyelids, tears overflowed and ran down her cheeks.

"Don't cry. Don't do that, please." He spread one large hand over the back of her head and pulled her to his chest. "Don't cry, my love. I'll try. I'll stay with you awhile. Oh, God, I'll stay with you. I can't stand this. I feel like my insides are being yanked out."

She threw her arms around him. "Oh, Ben. Yes, stay. Do. At least for a while. You'll get to like it here, I know you will. And the house, Ben. You'll love the house. It's big and out of the city a ways. There are fields and horses and trees, almost like Montana. We won't have to live in the city. Oh, Ben, just think, the two of us there. Together. Oh, Ben."

She held on to him so tightly he could hardly breathe. He rocked her back and forth gently. He would do anything for her. Anything.

"I love you, I love you," he just kept repeating.

Maybe that by itself would be enough to sustain him in this strange land. Having her, holding her, watching her awaken beside him each morning. Perhaps that would make up for living in a place he despised even though he hadn't even laid eyes on it.

Four

Ben disliked Andrew Drewhart from the very moment Dessa introduced them. He would have been disappointed if he hadn't. As for how Andrew felt about him, Ben couldn't tell, nor did he much care. The man treated him with cool civility, when he acknowledged his presence at all. It wasn't dislike so much as total dismissal. Ben might as well not have existed. Andrew, after all, had Dessa, didn't he? That's how he treated her, anyway, like a possession.

It might have been best if Ben had let Dessa settle the problem and stayed out of it, but he was, after all, a man of the wilderness. Dessa's friends would expect him to act uncivilized, wouldn't they? He decided not to let them down.

"You will, of course, stay in town until this dreadful business is settled," Andrew said as he directed the loading of Dessa's luggage on the rack of a shining black carriage. It was a handsome vehicle appointed with brass fittings and striped in gold. Ben had seen nothing so fine. A coachman sat up top and two seats inside faced each other.

Drewhart had already hugged Dessa and patted her, telling her how dreadfully sorry everyone had been to hear of her parents' passing.

He talked that way, Ben decided, because he had learned it somewhere. No one would use such words as dreadful every time he opened his mouth unless someone said they should. Ben helped the porter from the train stack the luggage and lifted one end of Dessa's trunk to place it on the rack of the carriage. How had she managed to come by so many possession during her short stay in Montana?

Andrew tapped his walking cane and watched with a sneer, clearly indicating his disdain at Ben for helping a servant. Dessa chattered on brightly to both men as if she hadn't a care in the world. Ben knew better. He sensed her nervousness at being with the two of them.

Andrew took her by the elbow and steered her into the carriage, then climbed in himself. Ben hopped up top with the driver. Dessa would have ample time alone with the man to explain to him just what was what, set him straight. Besides, Ben wanted to get a good view of this city, this place where the woman he loved had grown up.

The buildings were quite tall compared to those out West, and there was a lot of stone and brickwork. The air smelled of the nearby river and the stink of too many horses in the streets. The dwelling of which Andrew spoke—Ben wasn't sure who it be-longed to— was located along a tree-lined street away from the business district but conveniently nearby. From the street, rows of steps led to rows of doorways, and he wondered how people were supposed to tell one from the other. He soon discovered the houses were numbered, which he thought mighty handy.

The carriage drew up in front of 212, and Ben leaped to the ground and opened the carriage door with a flourish. The scowl on Andrew's face cheered Ben considerably. The man handed Dessa out and Ben caught her up in his arms, whirling her around and around until she squealed with delight.

"Welcome home, my lady," he said, then favored her with an impish grin and kissed her square on the mouth.

She wrapped her arms around his neck and kissed him back, right there in front of Andrew and the coachman and anyone else who happened to be looking.

"Did you tell him?" Ben growled in her ear. "Did you tell him you're mine?" He rubbed his nose on her neck and nibbled with his lips. "If you want, I'll pop him one, settle him down."

"Ben, behave yourself. This isn't Virginia City." She giggled, pushed out of his arms, and straightened her hat, which had been twisted askew by his antics.

He grabbed her hand and pulled her up the steps, ignoring the luggage the coachman had piled nearby. "Well, come on, show me around. I want to see where we'll be living."

"Ben, hush, please."

"What, Dessa?"

Andrew followed them to the door, looking peckish. "Dessa, I'm afraid I really don't understand what is going on."

"Didn't you tell him, dear?" Ben asked in a fussy voice he hoped matched Andrew's tone, though he had to admit he laid it on pretty heavy.

"Tell me what?" Andrew asked.

He had produced a key from his waistcoat pocket and unlocked the door before asking the question, and now he stood poised in the opening, peering out at both of them.

The bastard was good-looking. Ben had to give him that. But he was just too damn slick, a namby-pamby. And what in the hell was he doing with a key? Was this Dessa's place or Andrew's?

"Well?" Andrew asked, having gotten no reply from either Dessa or Ben.

"There will be plenty of time to talk later, Andy," Dessa said, patting his arm soothingly and stepping past him. She took a deep breath and let it out slowly.

She ignored Ben, who was now glaring at her, willing her to look at him. She hadn't told Andrew about the two of them, and it was obvious he wanted to know why.

Andrew said, "Clarice had the place aired out and brought in flowers after we got your first wire. I'm afraid they're not as fresh as they could be, considering you are a day later than you thought. Was there an accident? Were you ill?"

"No, nothing like that," she said, striding through the hallways and pulling off her gloves, which she had only donned for the last leg of the trip from Kearney.

Ben thought her demeanor somewhat changed, but he couldn't quite put a finger on what it was. He hoped she wouldn't become as prissy as Andrew after she'd been around him awhile. It was enough to make you puke, the way the man simpered.

"The trip was dreadful," she finally said, then turned and posed in the sunlight coming through the window.

Ben cringed and eyed Dessa. Dreadful? Now she was doing it.

"And I just couldn't continue without a bath and some sleep. Those trains throw everyone all together like cattle. And of course the day coaches are much worse than our first-class coach. But we all ate together at the stops."

Her voice faded as she stepped from the hallway through a large arch and into another room. Andrew followed her, occasionally throwing in a dreadful of his own. Ben wondered if he was just imagining the change in Dessa. Maybe it was something in the air. It was like she walked through the door of the train station onto the streets of Kansas City and became another person. Well, she didn't really become so much another person, as she reverted to the one who had first ridden into Virginia City beside him. Back before she learned of her parents' death and before she met Rose and Wiley and Maggie. Before she became a real down-to-earth, honest-to-God woman.

Or maybe, thought Ben, just maybe it had all been his imagination. A thing he wanted so badly he made it so. Her becoming a sweet, caring, and beautiful person he could love. The kind of girl who would save the life of someone at the risk of her own. Saving someone who wasn't even particularly likable and who wore ragged clothes and spoke with a foreign and quite uneducated brogue.

Dessa stuck her head through the doorway. "Ben, come on, come on in. I want to show you around the place."

"Oh, will you be staying?" Andrew asked, drawing up his mouth so that his styled mustache twitched.

Ben glared at Dessa once again, but she paid him no mind at all.

"Well, yes, he will," she said gaily. She looked Andrew right in the eye and grinned like she'd swallowed a sweet. "And we need to talk, Andrew."

She glanced at Ben.

He glowered and she smiled again. "But not here, and not now. I'm so tired, all I want is a hot bath and a nap. Come to dinner tonight, Andrew. Seven o'clock?"

Andrew glanced from Dessa to Ben and back to her. "When will you speak to Cluney?"

"Tomorrow is soon enough for business, I would think."

"And…and what are you intending to do about the business? You need someone with experience, someone at the helm who is an expert in financial matters as well as merchandising, Dessa dear, unless you want your father's beloved business to go right down the gutter."

"I said tomorrow, Andrew. Tonight is for something far more important."

"Important?" Andrew raised his fine brows.

"Yes, Andrew. Important to Ben and you and myself as well."

"More important than your father's business?"

She glanced at Ben again, and he saw a glimmer of the Dessa he had known back in Virginia City. She was there, in the flash of the green eyes and the toss of her noble head, but most of all in the warm smile she gave him. Then she turned to Andrew and answered his question.

"Yes, Andrew. More important than daddy's business."

Andrew was not happy when he left, warning Dessa that it was extremely improper for her to have this man—he gestured like he smelled something horrible—under her roof, she being a young single woman.

Dessa had only laughed. "Ah, Andrew, sometime you must go out West, and get some of that proper nonsense blown off you."

Andrew chose not to pursue the matter, but went off grumbling.

Dessa turned from the slammed door and opened her arms. "Come here, my darling, you look as if you've been run over by a herd of those wild buffalo you told me about."

"That wasn't a buffalo, it was a citified weasel. Dear God, Dessa." Then he burst out laughing and went to her, hugging her tightly and lifting her off the floor. He swung her up and tucked one arm under her knees.

"I don't want to forget how to do this, just in case you need me to tote you somewhere again," he said with a laugh, and carried her up the stairs.

Dessa held on to him tightly. Could it be true that she could have all this and Ben, too? Could God really be that kind to her? And why not? After all, he had taken her parents and Mitchell from her, hadn't he? It was about time something good happened in her life again.

"Where's your room, my lady?" Ben asked at the top of the stairs.

"There, kind sir," she said, and pointed dramatically.

She worked the latch on the door and he stepped inside with her.

He stopped and gazed with awe at the draped and bedecked, floral rose and cream and green room. "Good Lord, Dessa."

The bed stood on a pedestal and was draped with yards and yards of fabric that fell in gathers from the canopy. A wardrobe in one corner was decorated with curlicues the like of which Ben had never seen in one piece of wood. Those same twists and turns were cut in the wood of a desk and two bedside tables. A screen stood across one corner of the large room, and painted on it were huge roses in deep pinks with rich green leaves, all so outsized that they were nearly grotesque.

Wallpaper matched the pattern on the screen, as did a rug that covered all but about a foot of wood floor around the perimeter. Ceiling-high windows were also draped to match the bed canopy.

"Do you like it?"

"Well—I—well, to tell you the truth, Dessa, it's a little— uh, a little...." He couldn't find a word and gave up.

"Plain old Victorian didn't suit me. It's very new, called Moorish, but I lightened up on the mixture of colors and all that cluttered look, like pillows and draped fabric all over the walls—"

She broke off the chatter, for she had seen the room as he must be seeing it, and was scandalized.

He still held her in his arms and he turned slowly, taking in the whole effect, as if that way he could soften the blow to his sanity.

"Oh, Ben," Dessa said. "I'm sorry. It's—it's terrible, isn't it? I never realized, but—"

"Don't be silly. It just takes some getting used to, that's all. Well, maybe a lot of getting used to." Just like everything else in this godforsaken place. He let the thought go, for he held what he wanted right there in his arms, and if this hideous room came with her, so be it.

With a whoop, he took several long strides, tossed her on the enormous bed, and jumped right up there with her.

And wouldn't Andrew, the smartass, think this was absolutely dreadful?

She laughed with delight and together they rolled around until they had thoroughly mussed the floral bedcover. They came to rest with Ben astraddle her, pillows propping her head. She gazed up into his face and pushed the tousled hair away from his eyes.

"You didn't like Andrew even a little bit, did you?" she teased.

"What's to like?" He kissed her wrist, then captured both and held them above her head with an easy grip, fiddling with the buttons of her dress with his other hand.

"He's been a very good friend. And he is truly a decent man."

"You mean he's not dreadful?"

"Ben, stop."

He gave up on the tiny buttons and slid his palm over one breast. "Stop what, my dear?"

"Talking like that."

"But it's the way Andrew talks, and the way you talked once. For a minute there, when we first walked in here, you took it up again."

"I did not." She closed her eyes and basked in his gentle caress.

He leaned close, whispered in her ear, "Did Andrew ever make you feel this way?"

Gasping, she nibbled at her lower lip and he leaned down to put his tongue there. Whatever answer she might have made was drowned in the kiss.

Clinging to this man who had created a new world for her, she soared to join the heights of his passion. A passion she'd had no idea existed until she met him. Would it survive here, where he was torn from his element? Lord above, she didn't know, but as he explored her fully clothed body with his hands and mouth, she prayed it would. For to discover such an ecstasy and then lose it would be tragic.

Ben fumbled with the hem of her skirt, pulled at the layers of petticoats, lay his warm hand finally and gently on her bare thigh. "Dessa, will you marry me?"

"Oh, yes, Ben." She wanted to scream that yes so loudly that people riding by outside would hear her declaration of love. A still, small warning tickled at her senses.

"Give it time, though, Ben. I want to marry you this very instant, but we have to be sure. We have to wait until we're sure you can live here. I know you've said you can, but suppose you absolutely hate it? Suppose you just can't bear it? Then what? I won't have you miserable for my sake."

"With you, how could I be miserable?" He said the words, but he took his hand away, smoothed back the layers of fabric, and moved to lay beside her, one arm behind his head. "I suppose you're right. We'll wait a day or two, but you know something?"

"What, Ben," she asked lazily, feeling a deep contentment for the first time since her parents had died. Everything would be wonderful, given time.

"We're going to have to do something about all these horrible flowers. It might be best just to move to another room. I'm not sure much can be done about this."

She laughed heartily, then thought of what she was doing,

lying in bed with a man in the privacy of her own bedroom and having a conversation about the decor as if it were the most natural thing in the world.

"You can have a guest room, a very plain one," she said primly.

"That might be best," he said, a twinkle in his eye. "I wouldn't want to smudge your reputation, even if we aren't up to anything too scandalous."

She couldn't help chuckling. Her parents and Mitchell, too, would have liked Ben on sight. They would have gotten along famously. And they would all have known they could trust this man with their daughter, no matter what.

She grabbed his hand, enclosed it in both hers. "Ben, will we have a lot of children?"

"Mmm. Probably. I'm lusty, you know."

"Oh, you are? I hadn't noticed."

"And you, what about you? Are you lusty, my dear Dessa?"

She snuggled up against him. "With you I am."

"And when are we going to break this news to dreadful Andrew, this news that we are going to have lots of children?"

"He's been a good friend, Ben. Please don't talk about him that way. I thought tonight at dinner. Oh, my goodness, I wonder if there's anything in the house to cook?"

"Who's going to cook?" Ben asked innocently.

"Well, I am. I can cook."

"I thought rich people didn't do their own cooking."

"We weren't always rich. Well, we're not even really rich yet. Not like the Vanderbilts"

"Yet? Do you expect to be richer than this?" He flung a hand around, indicating the room he found so distasteful. "What exactly do you want?"

She stiffened at the tone of his voice. "Well, don't make it sound like a sin to have money."

He sighed and sat up on the edge of the bed. "Well, I didn't mean to. But to always want more and more no matter what you have... well, that's called greed."

"And how do you think this country got where it is? It wasn't led there by men who are content to sleep under a wagon all their lives." As soon as the words were out of her mouth, she wanted to take them back.

When Ben didn't reply, she crept across the bed and knelt behind him, laying her head against his rigid back. "I'm sorry. I didn't mean that. I just don't like you criticizing something you know so little about. My father worked hard all his life. His father started with nothing and together they built this business out of sweat and tears, and I won't have either of them reviled. But I didn't intend to be mean to you."

He let out a breath he'd been holding. "I'm sorry, too. Let's talk about cooking supper... I mean dinner. I'll help, but I hope you aren't going to pick any weeds to put on the plates. I have trouble figuring out what to do with that stuff."

"Weeds?" she asked, at a loss to know what he was talking about.

"Back there in Kearney. I distinctly remember my plate having weed heads right on the food."

"Oh, Ben. Ben." Dessa slid around and hopped off the bed. "That wasn't a weed head. It was parsley."

"What are you supposed to do with it?"

"Lay it aside."

"But why put something on a plate that no one can eat?"

"Well, actually, you can eat parsley, but no one does."

He eyed her and made a face. "Oh, well, then. That makes perfect sense."

She grabbed his hand. "Come on, I can see you've got a lot to learn about the kitchen. That is if you're serious about helping me cook. Most men aren't interested."

"Well, I cook beans over a fire. I even learned to fry fatback out of defense. You've tasted Wiley's." He followed her down the stairs and let her lead him to the back of the main floor where the kitchen waited.

Andrew arrived promptly at seven o'clock with his sister Clarice. She was tall and thin, one of those pale blonds whose skin is the color of flour and looks as if it would go up in a pouf at the slightest breeze. It was soon obvious that Andrew had hopes that his sister would absolutely charm Ben until he wouldn't pay any attention to Dessa at all. Clarice fell to the task with a fervor that made Ben very uncomfortable. He had never been actively pursued and wasn't sure how to handle it. Dessa was either at a loss as to how to help him or was amused by his plight. He actually couldn't tell.

Following a leisurely meal, Dessa fetched a flat metal disk punched erratically with holes, opened the music box, and inserted it. She wound a crank and out came tinkly music similar to that of the cremona in the Golden Sun. Ben had never seen such a thing, and went to inspect it.

"Andrew, will you dance with me?" Dessa asked coquettishly, and watched Ben squirm when Clarice arched a fine brow in his direction.

Andrew turned away from the music machine. "I don't dance, never did," he said too loudly and to no one in particular.

With a secret smile, Clarice took his hand. He gazed at the fragile and pale flesh. Blue veins lay just under the skin and he was afraid to handle her. She might shatter.

"Well, then," she said in her sophisticated back East accent, "I'll teach you. I'm very good at that."

She smelled of sweet powder, a heavy cloying odor that caused Ben to sneeze when she placed herself carefully within the circle of his arms. He did not want to do this, and he glared at Dessa as she and Andrew whirled gracefully in a wide circle around him and his partner.

"Relax, Ben," Clarice said. She held him at arm's length, her right hand on his left shoulder. "Put your hand on my waist," she said, and took his other hand in her left one. "Now, we'll just stand here a minute and sway with the music. No, no, don't look at your feet. Look at me. And sway. Like this."

He did that awhile, still trying to figure a way out of his predicament. He felt plumb silly. Maybe the music would end. Under his touch Clarice was as fragile as autumn leaves, dry and crackly, not warm and moist and sweet like Dessa. If he wanted to dance at all, which he didn't, it would be with Dessa, not this wisp of a woman who might break at any moment.

Without warning she began to move, dragging him with her.

"It's called a waltz, Ben," Dessa said as she and Andrew swooped past once again. "Get into the spirit. It'll be fun."

He thought of the drawn-out, boring meal, and how he kept waiting for Dessa to announce their plans to her old beau, and how she hadn't even come near the subject. They had spoken of the August cotillion and what the "gang" had been up to while Dessa was away.

Then they had talked about past galas given by someone named Annette and her sister Jeannie, who must have been famous for throwing outlandish parties. Still the subject didn't come around to Dessa and Ben. Now, here they were dancing—well, more or less—all over the parlor and still no sign she would break the news. Was he going to have to do it?

He stumbled and shuffled, and could not get the hang of the dance step. Clarice slipped agilely from him to demonstrate alone. How very elegant she looked, turning high on her toes, arms lifted gracefully, head thrown back like a long-necked white swan. Her filmy skirts floated out around her, lacy and cloudlike. Surprisingly Ben found the solo dance quite erotic, and when he glanced at Dessa, he saw that she and her partner had stopped and were watching with equal fascination.

The music ended and all three applauded. Clarice bowed self-consciously. "I guess I got carried away."

"You should have been a dancer," Dessa said. "In the ballet theater."

Clarice glanced quickly at her brother, then away.

"She wanted to be," Andrew said. "Father wouldn't let her. He said absolutely not. I think it broke her heart."

Two bright red spots bloomed on Clarice's pale cheeks.

"Well," said Ben. "Nothing can stop her dancing here in the parlor, can it?" He went to her, took her hand, and said, "Show me again, would you?"

Tears lay pooled in Clarice's eyes and she gave him a grateful look before replacing his hands and going through the steps patiently once again. He followed along, trying to feel the music like he felt the beauty of a Montana sunrise or experienced the awe of a crisp winter morning so quiet he could hear the beat of his own heart and the silent fall of snowflakes in the pines.

And then, almost miraculously, his feet got the message, and he and his partner tried a wide whirl. Dessa had rewound the music box, and stood beside it watching Ben with a dreamlike smile on her face.

He moved like a graceful animal, once his inhibitions were shed, and she found herself longing to dance with him, but not at arm's length and proper like with Clarice. No, she wanted to nestle in the curve of his long body, place her thighs against his, press her feverish flesh to the tight, supple muscles across his stomach. What would it be like to dance naked together, bare breasts to bare chest? The thought flittered through her mind so quickly it slipped away. She had no idea where it came from.

Perhaps it was past time for the two of them to marry. Thoughts such as she was having were certainly not proper, and couldn't be carried out between the two of them while they were unmarried. So why did she still feel such hesitance? Some vague feeling of unrest warned her the time wasn't quite right. There were things yet to be finished, but for the life of her she didn't know what. That admission reminded her that she had a dreaded task yet ahead of her, and she forgot the beauty of the dance. She had to tell Andrew that she loved Ben, not him, and that his long, patient wait had been in vain.

Surely Andrew had guessed as much by now. Even so, she hated to have to tell him. She would do it soon, in fact as soon as the music finished playing. Should she do it alone with him? Send Ben and Clarice into the library, or take Andrew there and leave them here? What a mess. She should have had this out of the way earlier. Alone with Andrew in the carriage with Ben riding up top would have been ideal, but she hadn't the courage. Andrew had been so glad to see her, so full of talk about how he had missed her and his plans for a future. Perhaps she'd hoped that if she put it off, Andrew would guess what was going on and bring it up himself. But he hadn't. Instead he had blatantly brought Clarice along as a partner for Ben, as if Dessa and Ben's relationship were entirely platonic.

The music wound down and stopped.

For an instant or two Ben and Clarice continued to move. Then they slowly came to a halt. Ben now seemed at a loss as to what to do with his hands. He held them in position for a while, then took them away and wiped his palms self-consciously down the sides of his pants legs.

Clarice smiled sweetly at him, and he forgave her everything she'd had in mind when she came into this house. She couldn't have known how he and Dessa felt about each other, or she would never have agreed to distract him for her brother. Surely she was much too kind a woman for that. He was silently grateful to her for teaching him to move around the room without stepping all over his own feet. He couldn't wait to dance with Dessa. How sensual it would be to hold her close and move about in such an erotic fashion. Just thinking of it made him want her terribly.

He glanced across the room to catch her eye and saw her take a breath that appeared to pain her. Then she laid her hand on Andrew's arm.

"Come on, we have to talk. I hope you two will excuse us for a little while."

With one hand tucked firmly under Andrew's elbow, she led him out of the parlor.

Five

Andrew was intent on holding Dessa's hands in his when they sat side by side on a sofa near the fireplace.

He lowered his lips to touch her flesh. "I've missed you so. I thought we'd never be alone. Clever of me to bring Clarice, wasn't it? I think they're getting along famously."

"Andrew... I have... uh, I have something to tell you."

He turned his eyes upward in a gesture she well remembered. It signaled that he thought she was going to say or do something he would find absurd.

Most of the time he was quite handsome, but he could always ruin it all with one of his ridiculous expressions. On the other hand, when Ben even glanced her way, she'd always get feeble in the brain and the knees. She had never expected such a thing to happen, except in her wildest romantic dreams. And who ever believed they would come true? She wished her mother had warned her.

"What is it, Dessa?" Andrew finally asked, when she just sat there staring into space and daydreaming.

She had almost forgotten what she was going to say to him, and had to think a minute. "What? Oh, yes, Andrew... uh, I have something to tell you."

He laughed uncomfortably. "You already said that. What is it?"

His expression this time told her he had finally guessed, or perhaps admitted to himself, what he should have known all along but was just too stubborn to acknowledge.

"Ben and I... we—"

Andrew leaned forward and put his lips on hers, quickly, almost harshly. "Hush. No, I don't want to hear it. You're just grateful. Sshhh. He saved your life, helped you when you were vulnerable. I won't hear this, Dessa. I won't." His fingertips tapped at her cheeks, but he didn't quite take her face in his hands.

She batted her eyes and pulled away. 'You must. Andrew, I'm so sorry. But I do love him."

"He's a lout. A nobody. What would your father think? Your poor dear mother?"

"Don't you dare do that, Andrew. Don't you do that. You know how much I loved them, how much they loved me. They'd want me to be happy."

He squeezed at her hands tightly so she couldn't pull further out of his grasp. His eyes took on a frantic, darting appearance. "My point, precisely, my dear. How in God's name do you think the likes of him can make you happy? He's a bumbling fool. What does he do for a living? I'll bet he can't even read or write. Whatever are you thinking of, my sweet?"

Andrew voicing the same doubts she'd felt herself upon meeting Ben sent chills up her spine. She shuddered and tears flowed from her eyes. Returning to her old life had quite confused her, made her unable to think clearly.

Andrew pulled a clean white handkerchief from his vest and patted the tears away. "Now, now. It's all right. You can't blame yourself. You were grieving and he took advantage of you, pure and simple. I'll just have a talk with him and set him straight."

Dessa came to her senses and pushed him away, tottered to her feet. "You'll do no such thing! This is my business, Andrew. Mine, do you hear? I'll not have you or Clarice meddling in my affairs. I loved my parents dearly, but they never wanted me to grow up and make any decisions, either. Now you want to take over where they left off."

"For obvious reasons," Andrew said, his earlier tenderness gone. 'You're about to make a terrible mistake that you'll pay for dearly."

"Well, then, I'll be the one to pay."

"Dear Dessa, sleep on this. Don't make your decision now. We have the meeting with Cluney in the morning. At least delay any rash promises you might make until after that. Speak to Cluney, listen to your father's will first."

Dessa glowered at him. "What do you know about daddy's will? I think you forget yourself, Andrew. And Clarice, too. And you tell her she can flit herself around Ben all she wants, he won't be interested." Dessa sniffled quite unbecomingly, whirled, and left Andrew standing there gaping at her.

In the other room Ben listened to the raised voices. A moment later he sensed Andrew in the doorway by the way Clarice cut her eyes in that direction.

"We'll be going now," Andrew said, his voice brittle.

Ben rose when Clarice did, turned in time to see Andrew's hateful expression directed right at him. Dessa had broken the news. Ben couldn't help giving Andrew a victorious smile, but felt icy feet treading along his backbone at the murderous glare he received in return. He'd best not turn his back on this one.

"Good night, Ben," Clarice murmured as Andrew draped her wrap around her shoulders and donned his own cape. Andrew fetched the black top hat from the hallway rack and hurried his sister out the door.

Dessa was nowhere to be seen when Ben turned. He went upstairs thoughtfully, slowing in front of her closed door. He wanted to tap on the elegant and shiny wooden panels, step inside, and hold her for a moment to say good night, but he didn't. If she wanted to speak to him, she would not have gone to her room in such a fashion. It must have been harder than either of them had imagined to tell Andrew they were in love.

He went on to his own room, making no noise on the carpet runner. After what seemed an eternity of trying to get comfortable on the thick feather bed, Ben crawled from the bed and stretched out on the floor. He'd slept on the ground most all of his life; learning to relax in one of those things would take some doing. Maybe it would be easier with Dessa lying beside him.

The meeting at the law firm of Cluney & Brown was scheduled for ten o'clock the following morning. When Dessa crawled from bed, the mantel clock had just chimed once and she was amazed to see it was only six-thirty. She hadn't slept well at all. If her brain wasn't dithering over what would be the best way to handle Daddy's business, it was echoing Andrew's words. One part of her wanted to be rid of the entire thing, wanted to flee back to Virginia City with Ben, and even on to California, if that's what he wanted. The sensible side, which she'd evidently left behind when she went to Montana, said keep the business, appoint Andrew to run it. In due time, marry him and settle down in a house out on the hill above the river. Have everything she had always wanted. Be his wife, the mother of his children.

But send Ben away? How could she forget that when Ben touched her, she caught fire with a passion she could barely control, or how his mouth devouring hers filled her with ecstasy. Together they had come so close to committing sins of the flesh. Though she hadn't yet let Ben know her in that way, how much longer would it be before she did? What a wicked and lustful woman she had become. Perhaps no better than the women who worked for Rose. She should either marry Ben this instant or send him away, but she couldn't seem to decide on either course.

She went to stand at the window, pulling the curtain aside to stare down into the street. Dawn chased at lingering shadows, tracing silver fingers along the walkway. A lone carriage moved over the cobblestones, the clip-clop of the horses' hooves fading into the distance. Leaves were tinged with autumn colors. Winter would soon arrive, roaring across the plains from the mountains of Montana, carrying in the wind vague reminders of that exquisite country. She missed it already. She missed Rose and Maggie, the little house she'd furnished so carefully, and Wiley's dry humor. She missed the glittering stars and the sky bigger than the whole world and bluer than any flower or lake or indigo dress, a horse between her legs, the wind in her face, Ben riding at her side. Placing wildflowers on Mother and Daddy's grave every Sunday after church. Lord, how she would miss it!

She let the curtain fall back in place, her mind a turmoil of indecision.

Dismissing the fact that she still wore her nightgown, she padded from her room and down the hall, stopping to tap softly on Ben's door before opening it. The room was dark, but her eyes were accustomed to the gloom, and she saw right away that he wasn't there. The bed hadn't been slept in, but a blanket lay in a pile on the floor. His boots and coat were nowhere.

Where in the world could he be?

A flaming sun lightened the sky, painting riffles of the wide Missouri River in splashes of pink and purple and gold. Ben drew in a deep breath, inhaling the unfamiliar odors. The town lay all around him, its streets and buildings, its people stifling him. There would be quiet sometimes, like now, but then something would bang and crash, someone would shout, dogs would bark. Noisy paddle wheelers and barges used the river as if it were a massive road, hauling all manner of goods. Some would eventually end up in the territories north to the Platte or Yellowstone all the way to the Great Salt Lake with their wares, and he wanted to swim out to one, climb aboard, and head in that direction with no more thought of Dessa Fallon and her precious Kansas City. Let her have Andrew and all the things she seemed unable to live without. That awful place with all the windows covered by thick draperies that cut out the sunlight, the very air he needed to live.

Ah, Dessa, dammit, how he loved her. He couldn't leave her here, and it seemed he couldn't get her to go with him, either.

With a sigh, he stuffed both hands deep in the pockets of his trousers and turned his back on the river. He would stay a while longer, see how things went. But he had made up his mind about one thing for certain. He could not live in this ugly world.

A familiar carriage waited in front of the house when Ben returned on foot some-time later. He went up the walk and opened the door carefully. The muffled sound of voices came from the library. What he wanted was to walk past the door and up the stairs without being seen, but as he drew nearer, tidbits of the conversation from inside—his name and Dessa's being bandied about—reached him, and he drew up against the wall. He couldn't stop himself from eavesdropping on the two people inside, for he recognized both voices from the night before. Andrew and his sister Clarice were in there and they were discussing him and Dessa, which Ben decided was surely his business.

"I understand her attraction to him," Clarice said. "He is quite handsome in a rugged sort of way."

Andrew snorted. "Rugged is being kind. I tell you, Clary, I will not allow this to happen. Fallon Enterprises is easily worth half a million dollars, and within a few years, with the railroads cropping up everywhere, a smart man could double its value."

"And you want to be that smart man, Brother."

"Oh, I will be, one way or the other. She's teased me since she was old enough to know the effect of her feminine wiles. I've waited a long time for Dessa Fallon."

"For Fallon Enterprises, I'd say."

"All right, I admit it. What's wrong with that? All our family has left is its name. Father and our no-good older brother have managed to squander all the money Grandfather left us. And you don't seem able to attract a suitable husband. What will you do when they take the house and what little we have left, Clarice? Go begging on the street? Or perhaps you'll dance for a living?"

"That wasn't very kind, Andrew."

"The time for kindness is long past, Sister. You'll help me with this or you'll starve, just as I will. Neither of us is equipped to make our way in this world."

"But I don't want to hurt Dessa. I've always liked her, even though she was a bit of a snob. Have you noticed how she's changed, how different she is?"

"Believe me, that's temporary. Let her get her greedy little hands on her share of the old man's business, let her realize how much money is involved, and we'll see how quickly she'll revert to her old ways. She was raised never wanting for anything. How long do you think she would put up living with that worthless no-good? Right now, it's just something new and different to her. Let her live in a house with cracks in the walls and no glass in the windows, let her spend winter out on the plains or in those dreadful mountains with little to eat or wear, and you'll see how quickly she would change her mind. Well, I don't intend to let it go that far, and you will help me."

"But Andrew. Even if she goes with him, she will have all the money. They won't have to live that way."

"Not all by a long shot, Sister, dear. In fact, it may not be enough. He's a money grubber, plain and simple. He only wants her for her money. He has a thing or two to learn as well." Here both paused.

Ben struggled to hold his anger in check. The nerve of the bastard. Admitting in one breath that he expected a share of Dessa's money, and in the next putting Ben on down the road. It was all he could do to keep from leaping into the room and socking that foppish son of a bitch right in the mouth.

But then Andrew went on, and Ben listened.

"You don't suppose he's already bedded her, do you? Dear God, if he has, she's spoiled somewhat, isn't she?"

Clarice laughed softly, bitterly. "I'm sure you'll be able to overcome that little scruple, Brother, dear. You've never been too particular about your own bed partners."

At that moment Ben thought he heard something and glanced up toward the landing. Dessa was standing there, gazing down at him, her features a mask of dismay. He had been caught skulking about, and there was nothing for it but to make the best of a bad situation.

"Good morning, Dessa," he called, and strode toward the stairs as if he had just walked into the house. "Did you sleep well?"

When he reached her, she studied him closely. "What were you doing?"

"Dessa, we have to talk, and now. Please."

He took her arm, but she pulled away. "No. Answer my question. Why were you eavesdropping down there?"

He ignored the question. "There are some things you need to know, and now, before you go to your meeting. What are those two doing here anyway? What do they have to do with your meeting this morning?"

"Andrew worked for Daddy. I thought you knew that."

Ben shook his head slowly. "How would I know that? And so what does it mean? That he has a part in the business?"

"He will have a say. He will advise me after we speak to our lawyer. Andrew knows all the ins and outs of Daddy's business. Much more than I do. I need his suggestions, his assistance. What's wrong with you?"

"Don't trust Andrew, Dessa. He means to—"

"No, I won't listen to that. Andrew has always been trustworthy. I've known him practically all my life. I may not be in love with him and that may be upsetting to him, but it doesn't mean he'll cheat me. I'm not going to throw him out of the business."

"I'm telling you, Dessa, Andrew is not to be trusted. I heard him and Clarice talking. They plan to—"

Dessa shoved his hand off her arm. A bright spot flared on each cheek and her voice tightened. "Ben, don't meddle in something you know nothing about. When this business is finished, then we'll talk about our future. Until then, why don't you just stay out of it?"

Ben jerked backward as if she'd slapped him. An ache closed around his heart. This was the Dessa he'd feared would return, the one he'd caught glimpses of when she first arrived in Virginia City. He'd thought that spoiled little brat long gone when the real Dessa appeared. The one who was compassionate and kind and forgiving. The woman he'd fallen in love with. Where had she gone in a flicker of an instant?

Before he could recover his voice, she hurried down the stairs, her action dismissing him like a servant. He watched her greet Andrew and Clarice in the hallway, and waited in grim silence while the three of them went out the door. The echo of its closing thrummed in his head. She didn't even look back; her desertion made him sick to his stomach.

Almost unaware of his actions, Ben rushed to his room, packed his few belongings in the small satchel, and hurriedly checked to make sure he had his money and return train ticket. All this in an unconscious flurry of anger and grief.

Down the hall, he paused at Dessa's door, which stood ajar, and pushed it open gently with his fingertips. Her nightgown lay across the unmade bed, yesterday's clothing was heaped in a pile on the floor, and on the dresser was a box of powder with a candy-pink puff.

He took a deep breath of the essence of her, closed his eyes tightly for a moment, then backed away. Her abandonment left him empty and bereft, much as the loss of his family had done so many years before. He might not be able to endure it.

Damn her, damn her to hell. How could she do this to him? Treat him in such an offhand manner and just walk away with orders that he be there when she returned so they could discuss their future. Well, she could forget that. This good-for-nothing territory bum would be long gone when Miss Dessa Fallon got back. And she could just deal with Andrew and Clarice and their schemes. They were all of a kind, anyway. All of a kind.

P. L. Cluney actually owned the law firm of Cluney & Brown, having buried his father's partner, DuBois Brown, three years previously. Old Mr. Brown died without heirs and so P.L. inherited the firm his father and his father's best friend had begun back in the old days. Before Missouri gained her terrible pre-war reputation, before the river became the road to the frontier, and before there were companies like Fallon Enterprises, the firm might not have been worth much. But today, ah, today that was no longer the truth.

As a practicing attorney, PL. didn't lower himself to appear in court to defend the scum periodically arrested for various and sundry common crimes. He'd learned where the real money in law was, and so he represented businessmen in their endeavors to become richer and richer. In doing so, some of the crumbs—well, a lot of the crumbs—fell or were coaxed his way. In Kansas City, P. L. Cluney was known as the rich man's attorney. If you wanted to earn money, and if you wanted to hide money, and if you wanted to keep money, you went to P.L.

He stood and greeted Dessa Fallon with a wide smile. The outcome of today's meeting meant little to him. Either way he would profit. With difficulty, he retained the smile when he shook hands with Andrew Drewhart and greeted his ghostlike sister. The woman gave him the creeps. She looked as if she had risen from the dead, and when she moved across a room, her skinny body appeared to float as if her feet didn't touch the floor. No wonder she had never married.

P.L. turned with relief back to the beautiful Dessa Fallon. At one time he had entertained hopes of his own where this lovely creature was concerned, but she apparently couldn't bear so much as his touch, so he had given that up, content now to simply get his share of her father's wealth.

He took his time opening the thick file he kept on Fallon Enterprises, pursed his lips as he leafed casually through the papers. Let them wait. In this office he was king and all their money couldn't change that. He knew well and good what he looked for and where it was, but he enjoyed making Drewhart sweat. He hated the simpering idiot.

The girl might be beautiful, but she was dumb when it came to business. Thank God, her father had known that, too. It made P.L. nervous to do business with Andrew Drewhart. He would have to tread very carefully. The man was a snake, no question.

He cleared his throat, glanced casually at his audience. "There is the matter of the will to be gotten out of the way first. As your father made me executor, I've been able to transfer funds and meet payrolls with no problem, seeing as how you were unable to return posthaste."

He glanced from under his disapproving frown straight at Dessa, then returned his attention to the papers. "Ah, here it is." Once again P.L. cleared his throat, and he began to read.

Dessa ignored all the whereases, and heretofores, scarcely listening to the drone of the dreadful man's voice. Daddy had left Dessa the farm and the house in town, as expected. Her mind wandered. She would soon be rid of Cluney, as her first act as the new owner of Fallon's would be to hire another attorney for the business. He was a detestable man, constantly putting his hands on her when she was no more than a child. She had always wondered what he held over her father's head.

Her ears perked up at the mention of Andrew's name. "... in total charge until such time as my son Mitchell is located or proven deceased."

"Mitchell?" Dessa cried. "Daddy believed he was alive?" She clasped both hands over her mouth.

Cluney glared at her. "Foolishness. Utter and complete."

He continued to read, his expression telling her not to interrupt again. But she did when he read, "My daughter Dessa will receive a monthly stipend based on a percentage of the net profits of the company as set down—"

"Wait. What does that mean?" She asked.

P.L. leered at Andrew, who smiled and leaned back in his chair.

"It means, my dear, that your father knew you would have no interest in the business. If you'll let me continue, his intent, I believe, will become clear."

"But Andrew… surely he didn't mean Andrew to have the business?" Her voice failed her. Mitchell alive? Andrew in charge of Fallons?

"Not entirely, my dear. Here, listen: 'From her half of the business, my daughter Dessa will draw a monthly stipend, a percentage of the yearly net income as recorded by said executor. The remainder of her half will be invested in a trust fund which will go to her in the event she marries."

Dessa interrupted. "But you said you needed me to return to handle the business, to… to decide if we should sell. You said you had a buyer and I had to come back to take care of it. You said…." Dessa rose from her chair, sending P.L. a blazing stare.

"I'm afraid I don't quite understand. I said nothing of the kind. I simply wired you the money you needed. Drewhart here said he would wire that you should come home for the reading of the will." Cluney sneaked a quick glance at Andrew. What had that scoundrel been up to behind his back? He hurried to smooth over the damage.

"Obviously, your father expected you and Mr. Drewhart to… uh… to marry, and that is why the will is drawn up this way. Husband and wife share equally, isn't that so? And it is really a moot point whose name the business is in, is it not?"

"And of course your father's belief that Mitchell would be found alive has proved unsubstantiated. Dreadful business." The attorney shook his head.

"That doesn't answer my question."

P.L. raised his thick brows. "I'm sorry, I didn't hear a question."

"Why did you continue to wire me saying it was imperative that I return?"

P.L. glanced at Drewhart, glanced back down at the open file, stared at the wall. This was no time to make an enemy of Drewhart when he was about to control Fallon Enterprises. By God, why didn't the man say something?

Dessa took two long steps to the desk and slammed her fist on it. "Sell the business. Now! I will have nothing to do with this... this *male* conspiracy. Sell it to whoever made the offer."

Andrew and P.L. glared at each other, both refusing to meet her accusation.

"There was no offer?"

Neither answered.

Dessa turned to Andrew. "You did this?"

Andrew licked his lips and caught at her arm. "Listen to me, Dessa. It was for your own good, dammit. While you were playing around with God knows what kind of people— the scum of the earth live out West, everyone knows that—I was keeping things going. Half the time when your father and mother roamed all over the country I took care of the business for them.

"It was me who built it into what it is. You didn't think your father had enough sense to do that, did you? And then he went off on that idiotic search for Mitchell when he should have been tending to his business. Buying a godforsaken failure of a store in a town destined to die. I told him, warned him, but he wouldn't listen. You see where that got him."

What was he saying? Search for Mitchell? He acted glad Daddy and Mother had been burned up! Hate roiled up from deep in her stomach. How dare he?

Andrew ranted on: "They were crazy, both of them. And look what happened. I could have told them as much, but they wouldn't listen to me."

Dessa scarcely felt the grip of his fingers, barely understood the meaning of the words. "What about Mitchell? What are you talking about? Andrew, answer me."

"Not you, too? Dessa, Mitchell is dead. Someone just wanted to blackmail them, that's all. Trick them out of some money. Listen to me. You and I will run this business together. Together we will grow very rich. Come to your senses, girl. Cluney, tell her."

Dessa yanked her arm from Andrew's tight hold and whirled to face Cluney. "Don't you say one word to me, you thief. I'll see you and Andrew out of my father's business for good before I'm finished. If either of you takes one penny you're not entitled to, I'll see you in jail. You understand me? In jail.

"And Andrew, I want to know exactly what was said to my parents about Mitchell, and I want to know this instant."

"Dessa, it was a scheme. That's all," Andrew said, his voice quavering. "You're angry at the wrong people. You should be shouting at the woman who wrote the letter and convinced your parents to go to that godforsaken place. It got them killed, girl. Think. We're not your enemies."

Clarice, who had not said one word, as was proper for a lady caught up in men's affairs, rose and took Dessa's arm. "You're distraught, that's all," she said soothingly. "Andrew, let me take her home. We'll call a doctor. She's not been well since that dreadful train trip from Montana. She needs to rest. We'll get the doctor to give her a sedative."

Dessa stepped back. Clarice had come along for just this purpose, to control her if she got out of hand. Andrew had thought of everything, and his sister, whom she'd thought of as a friend, had become his willing accomplice.

Dessa pulled from the fragile hold Clarice had on her. "I am not distraught about anything but this clever little scheme the three of you have cooked up. I don't want you in my home, any of you. And I'm seeing another attorney as soon as I can. You haven't heard the end of this."

She left the office, stalked across the anteroom and out into the hallway, where she paused to lean against the wall and catch her breath. Anger swelled within her like a pot about to boil over. She had to get away from them. She had to think about what to do. She had to find Ben!

Six

Ben walked all the way downtown to the Union Pacific train station. He figured he could have hailed a hansom cab, but he was so angry the inside of a cab wouldn't have contained him. He needed to gesture and swing his arms and eat up yards with his long legs. Twice he made a wrong turn and had to ask directions. Finding his way in the city was a bit more difficult than out in the wilderness. There one only had to know east from west, north from south, and sometimes only up from down. Here matters were much more complicated. There were unfamiliar street names and alleys that led nowhere and had to be backtracked.

But he finally reached the impressive stone and glass structure of the station. He hurried inside, where a clerk informed him that the train bound for Kearney with connections west was at that very moment standing on the track. If he hurried, he could make it.

Steam hissed around his legs as he leaped aboard the last passenger car. The train jerked, hooted, clanged, and hissed into motion. He remained on the rear platform, hanging on to his satchel with one hand and the railing with the other. Soon Kansas City disappeared into the distance, and he watched until the buildings were only an ugly growth on the horizon.

He turned away then and let out an explosion of breath that carried a world of pent-up anger and frustration. Much as he hated leaving Dessa, he must face the inevitable as he had been forced to do time and time again. It was nothing new to him to have all he loved snatched away One day maybe he'd learn to keep a distance from such entanglements, if he lived long enough. As for Dessa, he had to let her go; she belonged in this place, he did not.

Inside the car, Ben found a seat and crammed his long lanky body into the space, fitting the satchel under his legs on the floor. He was going home. Like Dessa, he needed to be where he belonged.

Dessa paid off the coachman and raced up the steps to the house. She jabbed at the keyhole several times before hitting it and unlatching the heavy wooden door. Inside she called out to Ben before she even slammed the door. When he didn't reply, she ran to the bottom of the stairs, called again, then started up, hitching the bronze shot-silk skirts above her shoe tops.

The echo of her own voice in the otherwise silent rooms scared her, made her heart thump all the harder as she trod along the carpeted hallway. The door to Ben's room stood open. What she already feared, she denied as she pawed through the empty armoire. The few clothes he had brought along were gone. In the drawer she found nothing. He'd had a small black satchel. It was nowhere, though she searched every corner and even under the bed. By that time her stomach was roiling and the backs of her eyes were burning.

"No, Ben. *Nooooo*," she cried, and flung herself across the bed. There was not even the smell of him there, and she remembered seeing the blanket piled in the floor earlier that morning. It was now folded awkwardly at the foot of the bed. She grabbed it up, buried her face in the folds, and breathed in his fragrance, all that was left of him in the empty room.

What had she done? Where had he gone?

There was no sense in asking such foolish questions. She already knew the answers. She had been cruel and stupid and unfeeling, and he had gone back to Montana.

She wasted little time crying into the blanket. Everything that had happened to her this morning, the innocent betrayal by her own father, Andrew's scheming, the dishonesty of the attorney the family had trusted—none of it mattered. What mattered was Ben Poole. He was kind and gentle, a man who had been hurt terribly by life, a man who had offered his love without strings, a man she had mistreated out of her own selfish desires.

Her heart ached for him.

"Oh, Ben, please forgive me," she cried, and tossing away the blanket, she raced to her own bedroom.

There would be no time for the trunk. She hadn't even unpacked everything yet. She jerked up the lid, intent on dragging out only the bare essentials to pack in her valise. There was no telling how many trains a day left Kansas City for Kearney, and she had no idea what their schedule was.

Rifling through the dresses, her hands touched crackly paper and she pulled from the folded clothing the package she had never opened. The one Walter Moohn had presented to her in that other life that seemed some distant dream. She ripped away the twine and paper, letting it all fall around her to the floor. And left in her hand was a stack of pictures and letters. On top was a tintype of Mitchell taken before he rode off to war.

She recalled Andrew's words about Mitchell and a mysterious letter. Was this what had taken Mother and Daddy out West?

Tears filled her eyes and she sank to the floor, skirts spreading out around her like a fall of autumn leaves. She touched her beloved brother's image with trembling fingertips. Another tintype showed the entire family, her skinny with braids, Mitchell looking all grown up at sixteen with his hair slicked down, Mother and Daddy stiffly posed like adults would do when faced by the formidable black-draped photographer and his paraphernalia. On closer inspection she saw that Mitchell's arm was around her shoulders, his fingers holding on to her as they stood in front of their parents.

It was almost more than she could bear, considering all that had happened in the past few days. For a long while she hugged the two pictures to her breast, scarcely breathing in her great sorrow. And now she had lost Ben, too, and not even a picture to remind her.

But there was. There was a picture. They had it taken at thousand-mile tree when they started back East together. The photographer was to mail the stereograph to her here after he returned to New Jersey. When would it come? How long would it take? She couldn't remember him saying, but she was sure he had. When it came, would that be all she would finally have of her lost love? Just like her brother.

Dragging herself away from such thoughts, Dessa laid aside the pictures and fingered through the letters. Two from Mitchell that she and her parents had read hundreds of times, and a couple Daddy had written when he'd been away from home, and one in a strange hand. The envelope was addressed to her father at Fallon Enterprises, Kansas City, Missouri. Just that and nothing more. There was a return ad-dress of Bannack, Montana. The letter Andrew had spoken of. It had to be. Dessa squeezed her eyes shut for a moment, took a deep breath and slipped out the single sheet of paper. She had never seen this letter before, and she was almost afraid to read it. For a while her hands shook so hard she actually couldn't make out the tight letters printed there, but she braced both arms on her knees and concentrated on each word in turn.

Sir,

This letter will probly come as a grate shock to you, but I deem it important as you will as well.

Yore son Mitchell did not die in the war. I know where he is and he is in great trouble, danger, I mean to say.

I only rite this in the hopes you will come to him, bring him some money so we can run away before they kill him. If you will come by train to Virginia City, Mont. terr. soonest, I will be in touch with you about how you can fine yore son. I repeat, he needs you badly.

My name is Celia Cross and I love him.

Best regards.

Dessa shook her head, wiped moisture from her eyes, and reread the letter. It still said the same thing. Mitchell was alive! Glory to God, Mitchell was not dead.

Celia Cross. Who was she? Why had no one in Virginia City said anything? Surely if they knew about Mitchell they would have told her. Had her parents spoken to this Cross woman? And if so, what had they learned? Had they perhaps found Mitchell?

No, that wasn't possible, for where would he have gone? He surely wouldn't have run away from her. What had happened? Oh, dear God, what had happened and where was Mitchell now?

She searched the sheet of paper for a date, found none. How long ago had this been? Certainly before her parents had made their hurried trip to Virginia City under the guise of business. Now she understood why they had gone. If only they had told her. But perhaps they weren't entirely sure the Cross woman was telling the truth, and didn't want her to get her hopes up. In truth, she knew they didn't tell her because they still considered her a child, had even arranged for that stupid chaperone to travel with her out West.

It hurt her terribly to learn that Daddy didn't trust her to run the business and had left it in Andrew's care. But in all honesty, before she had gone west, before she had met Rose and Ben, perhaps she would have been content to marry Andrew and let him handle the affairs of Fallon Enterprises. That was changed now, though.

Frantically, she gathered up the pictures and letters, climbed to her feet, and stuffed them in her valise along with a couple of dresses, some spare underclothing, an extra pair of shoes and gloves. She must hurry to the bank and cash a draft, for she had spent most of her money on the trip from Montana.

In the bank, Dessa stared with disbelief at the teller. "What do you mean, the account has been closed? It is my account. Who could do a thing like that?"

"I'm sorry, Miss Fallon. It's something to do with probate."

"This can't be. That's my money and I want it now!

"Ma'am, please. I'll call the manager."

"Yes, you do that. You do that this instant."

After being led to the dark and stuffy office of a fussy little man who said he was a vice president, Dessa refused to be seated. She chose instead to pace back and forth in front of the condescending man's huge desk. A plaque said *HORACE GREENWALLER, VICE PRESIDENT.*

Greenwaller had a high, ineffectual voice. "You should speak to Mr. Cluney. He is, or was, your father's attorney, and the executor of his estate. We here at the bank have nothing to do with the accounts. We can only open and close them under directions from our clientele. Surely you must understand that."

"That's drivel, pure drivel. I want my money now, or I'll see you before a judge," Dessa shouted.

"Please, madam, don't get hysterical. Would you like me to call someone?"

"I'd like you to give me my money, every cent of it. I'll never set foot in this bank again."

"I'm afraid that's impossible. There is no money."

"This is a bank, isn't it?"

"Well, yes, of course. But—"

"Then give me some of the money you have here."

Greenwaller pinched at his mouth with pink, soft fingers. It was plain to see he wasn't used to dealing with a demanding woman, most especially one who made absolutely no sense. But Dessa was past making sense. Andrew had done this to her, thinking to make her a prisoner until she gave in to his demands. She wondered what he really wanted, the business or her. It might be interesting to find out. Anger gave way to grim determination. If she couldn't get the money here, she knew where she could get it. Bargains were struck all the time in her world, and she had one to offer Andrew Drewhart, the self-righteous, uncouth swindler.

"Madam, are you all right?" Greenwaller asked.

"Oh, yes, sir. I am indeed all right. But you, sir, had best be looking for another job, because when I finish, that's what you'll be needing."

She whirled and left the office, her full skirts sweeping over a spittoon as she hurried from the bank.

The hansom cab took her to Andrew and Clarice's extravagant three-story home overlooking the river. She asked the driver to wait, and without bothering to knock, shoved open the door and barged in.

"Andrew... Clarice," she yelled at the top of her lungs.

Clarice rushed into the massive entryway, eyes wide and face pale. Before the two women could speak, Andrew emerged from another room.

"Dear Lord, Dessa. Did you learn such manners out on the frontier?"

"Manners be damned, sir!"

"Dessa, my word, your father would turn in his grave."

"Don't mention my father, you cad. You're not fit to utter his name, nor mine, for that matter. I want my money, every cent of it, and I want it now."

Andrew shrugged and smiled. "I have no idea what you're talking about, my dear. You need some money. Here, let me...." He paused and pulled a clip from his inside shirt pocket. "How much did you need? Enough to pay cab fare? Or buy a new dress? Here." He thrust a bill at her, smirking with self-satisfaction.

Dessa slapped the bill away. "I want the money that was in my account at the bank, and I want my first month's stipend." She snarled the last word, spitting it out as if he had a foul taste in her mouth, which indeed it had.

Andrew widened his own eyes in innocence. "I'm afraid until the will is probated, that isn't possible. Now, why don't you go into the parlor with Clarice and I'll bring you a brandy. It will quiet your nerves."

"I will not go into your parlor, I will not sit with your sister, I will not remain in this house one minute longer than I have to."

She fastened a thoughtful glare on Andrew and he gazed back at her, not giving an inch.

"Bring me a paper and pen," she snapped.

"What?" Andrew looked around as if she were talking to someone else.

"I'm going to sign over half the business to you. Free and clear, this very instant. No ties to that thief of a lawyer, no courtrooms or judges. Simple as that."

Andrew's jaw dropped, his eyes popped. Clarice uttered a tiny sound like a kitten mewling.

"Well?" Dessa demanded.

'You don't mean it. It won't be legal."

"Of course I do, and of course it will. I'll sell it to you for a dollar. That will be legal and binding. Technically it belongs to me, even though you and that scoundrel intended to pretty well bleed me dry before I get my hands on it. Am I not correct?"

"I don't know quite what to say."

"I'm sure you don't. Paper, pen." She snapped her fingers at him. "Move, Andrew, or so help me I'll fight you both. I'll go to New York and get a lawyer who'll make Cluney look like a hound pup, and you'll none of you have a cent. I swear I will, if I have to bankrupt Fallon Enterprises to do it."

She narrowed her eyes. "And think about this. If Mitchell is alive, I'll find him and then you'll get nothing. And even if he's not, I intend to marry Ben Poole as soon as possible. Either way, you've lost, you high-handed bastard. At least this way you'll have half, bought all legal and proper."

Andrew backed into the room from which he had just come, gazing at Dessa as if she'd gone quite daft. She waited a moment, then followed him, sensing Clarice padding along behind her making small simpering sounds down in her throat.

Dessa took the pen Andrew offered, dipped it in ink, and began to scrawl across the paper. When she was satisfied with the wording, she read it aloud.

Andrew was speechless. She was indeed selling him sole ownership of one half of the holdings of Fallon Enterprises free and clear, to revert to her only in the event of his death. And all for the sum total of her current account at the bank.

"Now," Dessa said in a softly menacing voice, "I'll sign this as soon as you reinstate my account at the bank. Oh, and by the way, we will drop by our friend Cluney's office and break the news to him. I'll want all the legal papers he's holding. All of them. I will be having an attorney of my own look things over and draw up further papers that will make this business deal airtight. I may only draw a stipend from the half that's left, but neither you nor that bastard will get your hands on any portion of it. I promise you, if you don't do this I'll fight you both until every dime is gone."

"Dessa," Andrew sputtered.

"Shut up, Andrew. Just shut up, and get your coat. You're coming with me. We'll just take this along and when everything is settled, I'll put my signature on it. I'm sure someone at the bank will witness it for us."

"What are you going to do, Dessa?" Andrew asked as they went out the door together, leaving a white-faced Clarice standing in the three-story entryway under a glittering chandelier.

"I've already told you," she said, and pushed away his hand when he tried to assist her into the cab.

He got in beside her, sighing deeply. "I mean after we do this."

"I'm going to Montana, Andrew. I'm going home to Montana."

Ben arrived at Devil's Gate exhausted. He'd slept very little, having spent even the dark of each night worrying about Dessa. If anything happened to her, he would feel responsible. He should never have left her in the clutches of that spineless Drewhart. Over and over he dozed off only to awaken with a start thinking he'd heard her call his name. He dreamed once of that night he'd heard that small, frantic voice calling out in desperation and rushed out into the darkness to find her near death but still fighting to survive. He awoke covered with sweat, despite the cold drafty air in the coach.

On the morning of the second day of his journey there'd been a prairie fire. It was as if the entire world were ablaze, from horizon to horizon. Soon smoke grew so thick no one could see or breathe. Far into the night passengers choked and gagged, finding little relief in the masks they fashioned for their faces. Even after the train passed through the worst of the smoke, the smell permeated every car. It had soaked into all their clothes until every movement wafted the odor up their nostrils once again.

Children cried incessantly. A pregnant woman at the front of the coach vomited over and over until a sour stench overpowered even the smoke. Her husband finally took her from the train at a stop where there was a doctor. Blessedly the conductor brought in buckets of water to wash away the vomit. Passengers rode with the windows open during the afternoon, but as they neared the mountains, the air grew too cold for that. Once again they were closed up in the overcrowded coaches, breathing each other's air and body odor.

As if that weren't enough, when Ben finally disembarked at Devil's Gate to inhale fresh air for the first time in days, he learned that the stage had been attacked by Indians and they were waiting for another to replace it before they could begin the trip to Virginia City. It might be another day and night, the clerk told him with a there's-nothing-I-can-do shrug.

Ben decided not to stay in a hotel, but instead walked over to the livery and asked if there was a horse he could rent.

"I ain't had a horse to let in a month of Sundays," the

man reported. One bony old sorrel gazed despondently at Ben from its stall.

"What's that?"

"You may call that a horse, I call it glue," the man said with a snort. "Tain't mine, in the first place; in the second place, it'd drop dead atween yore legs afore you was five mile out a town. Best you just bed down and wait for the stage."

"If you want, you can lay in the hay back yonder. Jest promise me you won't steal old Eb."

Despite all that had happened, Ben couldn't help giving the fellow a wry smile. "I've done a lot of things in my life, but I ain't never stole as sorry a horse as that."

The old man chuckled. "You'll be staying, then?"

"I appreciate the offer. I've got money, I can pay. I just don't take to hotel beds real well."

"Well, I can understand that, I surely can," the old man said, and took the coins Ben held out. "Stay till the stage comes. You can bathe in the horse trough, old Eb won't care one whit."

Ben thanked the man, tossed his valise in the hay, and dropped down next to it. He would wait till dark to take the old man up on the bath. Wouldn't do to get caught out on the street in the altogether by any of the gentler gender.

He must have fallen asleep, for he dreamed that Dessa lay in his arms, and he turned his face into clouds of her dark, sweet hair.

She touched him with her soft fingers. "I love you, Ben Poole."

"I love you, Dessa," he whispered, then moved his mouth down the side of her neck, lips coming to rest in the hollow of her throat.

Her bosom heaved and he nuzzled at the cleft between her breasts.

Miraculously, she was naked in his arms. The warm, moist

flesh tasted sweet as honey to his tongue. He lapped at the flavor, kissing an erect nipple.

She cried out, thrust the breast into his mouth, and arched against him.

Hands cupping her buttocks, he pulled her to his rising manhood, and moaned in ecstasy. Moving to the other breast, he rose to straddle her, and she opened herself to him.

Smooth as silk, he slid inside her surging heat and clung to her. She was his very life, she fed his soul. Together they were complete; apart from her he was nothing but a man content only to survive.

"I will never leave you," he cried out as he reached the pinnacle and tumbled over.

The dream turned nightmarish and she began to scream, begging him to help her. But he had gone on without her, and when he turned to take her hand, to save her, she was gone.

"Dessa, no." He sobbed, and stumbled. He would surely fall over the edge of eternity. Alone forever.

With a shout he bolted upright, cried out, and woke himself. It was the black of night and he was alone. Despite the chill, sweat soaked his back and under his arms. A horse snorted softly. Breath coming in short gasps, he smelled hay and manure and leather, and remembered where he was. Tickling at his nostrils was the burnt smoky smell from the prairie fire he'd ridden through. It was in his clothes and his hair and his skin.

Making love to Dessa in the dream had been so real he felt dizzy with it, even though he was fully awake. It was as if she had reached out to him from far away, and given herself to him so he'd know how much she loved him. So he would realize that he loved her. He could still feel her lush bare limbs wrapped around him, her warm sweetness when he buried himself deep inside her. How stupid of him to think he could deny love, the most precious of gifts a man and woman can give each other. He had to go back to her. Life takes so much from a man, he would be wise not to throw away what few chances it offers for happiness.

Trouble was, he didn't have enough money for a return ticket on the train. Time was when Ben Poole wouldn't have worried much, he would simply have taken what he needed. That's what the war had done to him. Made him a thief and a sorry excuse for a man. A killer, even. There had to be another way. To do such a thing now would be to betray the woman he loved, and that wouldn't do at all. He would find another way to get back to Kansas City.

He sniffed his smoky odor and decided to use that horse trough first. Come daylight he would tackle his other problems. No doubt there'd be a poker game in town, and he'd been known to win some hefty pots. Had lost some, too, he thought wryly, but let that go. He had very little left to lose.

The air was so cold he could see his breath when he stepped from the livery barn into the moonlit night. Looking quickly around to make sure no one was about, he slipped off his dirty clothes, carefully hung the clean spare pants and shirt over the hitching post, and stepped one foot into the trough.

"Holy cripes," he gasped when the icy water rose above his calf.

Gritting his teeth, he eased in the other leg and lowered himself very slowly into the wooden trough. It was all he could do to keep from shouting from the cold. He made do with a quick rub. Seeing as how he had no soap, it was certainly not a proper bath, but it would have to do. All the same, he rinsed some of the smell off, washed his hair as best he could, then climbed out.

He hissed through his teeth and danced about on the boardwalk to warm up, thinking how funny it would be if someone glanced out a window about now and saw a naked man doing a jig in the moonlight. Probably just think he was drunk and go on back to sleep. And he was drunk. Totally drunk with the need to be with Dessa, drunk with the realization that he was not complete without her, no matter where he was.

Dessa boarded the Union Pacific train that left Kansas City the next morning after Ben's departure. She would be just a day behind him all the way across the prairie, if indeed he had headed back to Montana. Once they passed through a wide bare gorge where a fire had burned itself out. During most of the second day they traveled through the ugliness of that sorrowful, blackened plain.

On the morning of the third day it began to snow, the flakes blown by a stiff wind that made the flakes look as if they were falling sideways. But on the ground is indeed where the snow landed. As the train pushed its way west, drifts piled up that threatened to block their forward passage. The storm let up by the time the mountains came in sight, the great blue-purple peaks stabbing through low-hanging gray clouds that lay like puffy skirts around their feet.

Occasionally Dessa would cry softly, staring out the window at the beauty of it all. Montana waited to cradle her and she wanted to throw open the window and shout, "I'm coming, Ben. I'm coming home." And silently she offered a prayer of hope. Let it be true, let Mitchell be alive like the letter said. Oh, please, God, let me find him.

Then at long last, when she thought she couldn't endure another minute, the conductor came through the car with his announcement. "Devil's Gate. Next stop. Devil's Gate."

Dessa let the conductor hand her off the steps down onto the platform of the station. Since she had only brought a small valise, she had carried it aboard, and now the conductor placed it beside her and tipped his hat.

"Hope you enjoyed your trip, ma'am," he said, and walked away, leaving her there with a scattering of other passengers on their way somewhere besides where the train was headed.

For just a moment or two she felt terribly afraid. Suppose Ben stayed on the train, went right on to California? Then what would she do? Whether she located Mitchell or not, she needed Ben, loved him, wanted him at her side.

Oh, dear God, suppose she never saw him again.

Seven

Ben blinked as he emerged from the darkness of the Devil's Hole Saloon. Clutched in his fist buried deep in one pocket was a roll of bills, enough to buy a ticket back to Kansas City, and he hadn't stolen it. Well, he hadn't exactly stolen it. The two yahoos he'd gotten into a game with weren't the best poker players he's ever seen; actually, it had been sort of like taking candy from a baby. Still, anyone who sits in on five-card stud ought to know the risks.

He blinked again to accustom himself to the brilliant sunlight and started up the boardwalk toward the train station. He wasn't paying much attention to people on the street; his mind was already on what he would say to Dessa when he arrived on her doorstep in Kansas City. So when he bumped elbows with a lady, he automatically tipped his hat and said, "Sorry, ma'am."

The lady stopped, called his name.

He took another look, recognized the voice in the same instant as he beheld her face, and grabbed Dessa around the waist, shouting at the top of his lungs and whirling her around and around so her feet flew through the air.

"My goodness, Ben. Oh, Ben." Her valise went sailing

and she wrapped both arms around his neck, laughing as they twirled faster and faster.

After a few dizzying seconds he staggered backward against the wall of the mercantile and buried his face in her neck. He held on to her tightly, not sure whether he should laugh or cry.

He had her; he wouldn't let go. Never. Never. Ben Poole, who thought he had shed his last tears over his family's graves when he was fourteen, felt warm moisture slip from beneath his tightly closed lashes. He kept his nose against her shoulder and inhaled her scent. How could he have ever walked away from her?

"Ben, you're squeezing me," she said gaily. "Oh, darling, I was so afraid you'd gone on to California. What are you doing here?"

He cleared his throat, but couldn't let her go, couldn't take his lips from her neck, her cheek, her mouth. She had called him darling.

Further, she let him kiss her, long and deeply, right there on the street in Devil's Gate, with one and all looking on.

That afternoon they boarded the stage for Virginia City, a long and arduous journey neither would much suffer from. They were happy to be alive and in love and together, no matter the conditions.

It rained much of the final day of their trip, so that they arrived in Virginia City as they had left, wading ankle deep in mud from the coach to the boardwalk. Neither had bothered to wire ahead, and the cold rain had driven everyone off the streets. It was a lonely, unheralded welcome.

"I don't know about you, but I'm ready for a bath and some sleep," she told him while they stood, shoulders hunched against the icy pellets of rain.

He looked around, shrugged. "Where?"

They both grinned and laughed. Where else?

Small valises in hand, they made their way toward the Golden Sun, dashing along and dodging sheets of water running from store roofs. They arrived inside the quiet hurdy-gurdy house soaked to the skin and looking and feeling like a couple of drowned rats.

Grisham scurried from behind the bar. "Sorry, we're not open yet."

Ben took off his hat and whopped it against his equally sopping pants leg. "It's us, Grisham. Dessa and Ben. Don't you recognize us?"

The lanky Englishman raised his thick black brows and peered at the drenched couple. "Why, so it is. So it is. Well, Miss Rose will be glad to see you. But she's out at her place today. Weather's been so bad we've had little business. If it hasn't been snowing, it's been raining, so she took some time off to rest. Truth be known, I believe she's trying to make up her mind about selling the place. Needs the quiet."

Grisham grabbed his apron up in both hands and wrung it in his hands. "We didn't expect you back so soon. But I'm sure it'd be fine with Miss Rose if you went on up to her rooms."

From up above on the landing came a shriek. "Ben. Oh, Ben, is that you?" Down the stairs flew Maggie, long hair waving behind her like a flag, and a thin robe opened wide and trailing along. Her breasts bounced curvaceously above a bright red corset when she threw herself into Ben's arms.

"I'm all wet, Maggie," he warned too late, then gave up and hugged her close.

"Does Rose know you're here? And Dessa, you did bring her back with you."

Dessa gazed a question at Ben. Bring her back?

"Well, not exactly, it's more like she brought me back. But

it doesn't matter. How is Rose, how is everyone? Grisham said something about selling the Sun? Is it true?"

Maggie shrugged and stepped back. "You're all wet. Come on upstairs, the both of you. We'll get some hot water so you can get cleaned up. What a trip that must be, up from Devil's Gate."

"It's a real bruiser. 'Course you ladies have a bit more padding, but I'll swear I feel like my bones have poked right through my rear end by now. I'd rather ride a horse across the whole country than that coach five miles, I swear I would."

Maggie chuckled and grabbed Ben's arm, swinging him around so she could look. She rubbed a hand over his butt. "Nope, no bones there. If you'd eat more, you wouldn't be so lank."

Dessa felt herself flushing at the sight of Maggie touching Ben so freely and so personally.

"Well, Maggie girl," he said, "I'd sure appreciate that bath and I know Dessa would, too."

"Come on up, then." Maggie stopped at the bottom step and glanced back over her shoulder at Ben and Dessa. "You going together or separate?" she asked with a wink.

Ben glanced down at Dessa, grinned at her flustered look, and winked back at Maggie. "Well, now, you'll have to ask Dessa about that."

"Ben," Dessa scolded. "Shame on you." Even as she spoke the words, she found herself wishing she had the temerity to throw caution to the wind. But she didn't. She had been brought up properly and decent girls didn't do such things. They only wished they could.

"Dessa can go first, then you can warm up her water for me," Ben said.

"Thank you so much, kind sir." Dessa executed a mock bow and headed up the stairs.

"I'll stay down here and see if I can talk Grisham into a cold one while I wait. Come on back down, Maggie, when you get Dessa settled. We can talk."

"Yes, okay, Ben, I will. I have a surprise."

Dessa followed Maggie thoughtfully up the stairs. She had never completely understood the relationship between this woman and Ben, or between Ben and Rose, for that matter. The entire situation puzzled her greatly. She wanted to know more about it.

During the long stage ride, she and Ben had discussed her financial problems with Andrew and how she had handled it. Ben appeared to have quite a head for business, making several suggestions for future investments in the territories that made good sense to her. She would definitely look into some of them. Ben had applauded her stance against the crooked Cluney and subsequent victory, though he did suggest immediately hiring another attorney to set matters straight.

She was pleased to learn that Ben had a natural affinity for bookkeeping and could keep numbers straight in his head without even so much as a piece of paper to jot notes on. That ability was something for her to consider. She had laughingly joked about hiring him to handle that part of the business, but on reflection she thought seriously that it wasn't such a bad idea. Not hiring him, exactly, but perhaps making him a partner. He had no money to put into the venture, but there would be enough money even after the sale of half the business to Andrew and Clarice. By law, Fallon Enterprises belonged to her and Mitchell, if he was still alive and she could locate him. Given a decent attorney, she should have no trouble getting things straightened out.

Then what she would need to run the business properly was someone with Ben's phenomenal ability with figures, since she had absolutely none in that area. Someone she could trust totally and completely. There was no doubt in her mind that Ben Poole was that man.

She had asked him where he learned to manage figures like he did. He just shrugged. "I guess I always knew it. I thought everyone did." He'd laughed heartily then. "It's like seeing colors and speaking the language. You just suppose if you can do a thing, then everyone else can, too. Especially if you always knew how to do it."

"I'm always doing Rose's books—she's such an absolute mess with numbers."

"That should have made you wonder. If Rose couldn't do it, there might be a few more people who couldn't," Dessa teased.

Ben looked at her blankly for a moment, then realized what she was saying and grinned.

Relaxing in the tub of exquisitely hot water, Dessa smiled at the memory. Some of the time Ben had such a wonderfully open expression, almost as if he were saying, Here I am, surprise me, make me laugh. Yet within the depths of his blue eyes dwelled a frosty barrier that he could throw up without warning, daring anyone to break through. She wondered what lay hidden there, and vowed to find out before much longer. There were definitely some questions that needed answering before they married. His relationship with Sarah Woodridge and the twins was a big one; Maggie and Virgie as well. She might share Ben with Rose, who was more like a mother to him, but she had no intention of sharing him with a widow or a couple of whores. Maggie said they were like brother and sister, but how did Ben feel? And what about Virgie?

But before any of that—before anything else, in fact—she had to try to find Celia Cross. If her brother Mitchell was still alive, then she would find him, no matter what it took.

On the trip back Ben had told her he would help search for Mitchell, but warned her not to have too much hope. He thought the entire thing sounded like an attempt to extort money out of her folks, and if she got involved it would amount to the same thing.

"Just promise me one thing," Ben had asked. "Promise me you won't go off on any wild goose chases. That if you hear anything, you'll come to me first, or even Walter Moohn. There are outlaws hiding out all over these hills. Some even worse than the two you encountered on your first trip out here."

She shuddered, remembering Coody and his sidekick. She'd almost managed to forget the incident, in view of everything else that had happened in the ensuing weeks since. Thinking back on that nightmare, she had been glad to promise Ben she wouldn't go off on her own.

If anyone would know where this Celia Cross lived, Rose Langue would, and she intended to bring it up as soon as possible.

The hot bath relaxed her so much she had almost dozed off, when Maggie tapped on the door. "We've brought water to heat the bath for Ben. Are you finished yet?"

She crawled from the tub and toweled down. "Just a second," she called, and slipped into the robe Maggie had laid out.

Despite her protests that she could get a room at the hotel, Maggie bundled her into Rose's bed and put up a screen around the tub so Ben could bathe in privacy. "That's nonsense. Rose won't be back before Friday. She would be pleased that you used her bed."

"I happen to know that your little house is waiting for you. She just shut it up like it was, said she was sure you'd be back soon. But it'll be cold over there today. You'll be needing to get yourself a stove. Old Mister Winter's tapping on the door, and you ain't seen nothing till you've seen him act up around these parts."

As if reminded of the cold damp weather, Maggie slipped a couple of sticks of wood onto the bed of coals in the stove and flipped the damper open. Soon a cozy, crackling fire warmed the room.

"I'll light a lamp, and then I'll just tell Ben he can come on in and take his bath. You need anything?"

Head already nestled into the pillow, Dessa stared with glazing eyes at Maggie. "No, I'm just fine," she murmured, and closed her eyes.

When Ben slipped into the room a few minutes later, he found Dessa asleep in Rose's big feather bed. He went to stand beside her for a few moments.

The hot bath had flushed her cheeks and left damp ringlets of dark hair around her face. He touched her tenderly, running the tips of his fingers over her cheek, down her throat, and stopping at the swell of her breast. He was overcome with such a longing for her he could scarcely stand it. Not just a sexual urge like the kind that made a man grow hard and throbbing, but a deep-down desire to live with her, to lie beside her, to sit at a table and take a meal with her, to brush her hair and scrub her back and run through the woods with her. To see reflected in her green eyes the same undying desire for him.

Quietly he bent and touched his lips to her warm cheek. Her long eyelashes fluttered, brushed at his chin, and she sighed a breath of air that caressed him gently. Ever so carefully he kissed her lips, then left her there to sleep while he bathed in the warmed-over water steaming with her feminine scent.

No woman had ever attracted him in such a way. He found himself in awe of his own feelings for her. A girl not of a class he thought would ever be attracted to him, and certainly not that he would be attracted to. She had some city ways that needed toughening up a bit if she were to live in the territory, but he had no doubt that she could handle whatever came her way. Her facing down Andrew and that sister of his had impressed Ben.

Maybe Rose was right. He and Dessa could cut a swath across this great new land the likes of which none had seen. With the coming of the Union Pacific, other railroads would open up the rest of the West. It was already beginning up north, and if they were careful and paid attention, he and Dessa could be ready for the movement of the rails, investing in businesses all across the land even before anyone else could guess their value for the future.

Ben lowered himself till the water lapped on his ears, and chortled. Who would have thought it? Who would have thought Ben Poole would ever care for anything but a Winchester and a blanket to throw on the ground?

He only saw one obstacle in their path right now, and that was Dessa's search for her brother. He'd have to try to find that Celia Cross and put the fear of the Lord in her. He wouldn't have the woman, whoever she was, messing with Dessa's mind, for he could see how much she loved and missed her brother. He decided to put a stop to this nonsense straightaway, so he and Dessa could get on with their lives.

Dessa awoke sometime in the night. From somewhere she heard a light snoring. Startled, she sat upright and self-consciously crossed her arms over both breasts. The noise was coming from the other side of the bed. She leaned over. It was so dark in the room, she just could make out someone lying on the floor all covered with quilts. It took only a moment to realize that Ben Poole was asleep next to her bed.

"Oh, Ben," she whispered. "Dear Ben."

She lay back and let her hand trail off the bed so that it rested lightly on the lump that she took to be his shoulder.

When she awoke the next morning, he was gone, the quilts folded neatly at her feet. She wondered if perhaps she had dreamed the whole thing.

Downstairs she learned that Ben had gone out on a freight run with Wiley. She was disappointed, having thought he wouldn't go back to work for the Bannon Freight Company. Certainly not the very next day after they returned, even before she could run down Celia Cross. She would need Ben.

"He said the old man had his ox in the ditch, and that you'd understand," Maggie reported.

Though disappointed, she did understand. It was Ben's habit to help where he was needed. She wouldn't have him any other way. She telegraphed that message to Maggie with a warm smile. "Well, I'm going to get my house opened back up. I'm sure it could stand a good airing. Looks like the rain has moved out for a while."

"Uhmm," Maggie said. "But it's a mite chilly out there today. Winter is definitely in the wind."

"Looks absolutely perfect to me," Dessa said. She started out the door, then turned back. "Maggie, do you know a Celia Cross?"

Maggie knitted her brows, then shook her head no. "Rose might, though. She knows just about everyone."

"I might just ride out and talk to her, if you think she wouldn't mind."

"She'd be real happy to see you."

"Where does she live?" Dessa asked.

"Oh, just a mile or so out of town. It's a little cabin surrounded by flowers. Roses. They're her favorites. The whole backyard's full of roses. She has water hauled to them in the dry months. It's a sight. Folks say she loves those roses better than most mothers love their babies. But they just don't know Rose real well. Rose, she loves her friends, those she takes in, like Tressie Majors, who's now Tressie Bannon, and of course Ben. And now you."

Dessa looked up sharply. "Me?"

Maggie nodded. "She was so afraid you wouldn't come back, I caught her crying the day after you left."

"Rose? Crying?" Dessa had thought the woman unrelenting in her toughness.

"You should have seen her when Tressie went off with that Reed Bannon. 'Course it's all right now, and once in a while she gets to see their babies. Just like she's their grandma or something." Maggie tucked her chin, then looked up brightly at Dessa. "And it'll be the same with me and Samuel. Oh, Dessa, we're getting married, and Samuel says we'll have lots of babies, and he's going to build me a house."

"Oh, Maggie, that's wonderful. When did all this happen?"

"While you and Ben were gone. Well, at least the part where we decided to get married. He used to come and dance with me, but he was so quiet, I never dreamed. And then one day he just dressed all up in his finest—we didn't even recognize him, me and Rose—and he came and asked for my hand.

"Oh, Dessa, do you think it's all right? A woman like me marrying and having a family? I'm so happy."

The girl rushed to Dessa, threw her arms around her neck.

"Sweetheart, I think it's wonderful if you love him, if he loves you," Dessa said with a laugh.

"Oh, I do, we do, he does." She broke out laughing, and whirled around and around.

Dessa got caught up in the girl's gaiety, and soon they were both chattering away about weddings and men and having babies.

"I don't go in the cribs anymore, you know," Maggie finally told her seriously. "It wouldn't be right."

Dessa kissed the girl on the cheek. "I wish you and Samuel the very best. You must stay in touch with Ben and me. Where will you live?"

"Samuel has a farm in Nebraska. He got the land from his older brother, who homesteaded it and then died."

Dessa nodded her head. A great weight had lifted from her shoulders. It was really true, then, that Maggie and Ben had a platonic relationship. And she was very happy that the woman had found love before it was too late for her to change her life.

After Maggie went upstairs, Dessa decided not to ride out to Rose's place, but to wait till the Golden Sun's owner came in Friday. She had plenty to do getting her own home livable in the meantime.

Ben didn't return until the next day, riding in with Wiley and hopping off the wagon in front of Dessa's. He swung the door open without knocking and stood in silence watching her sweep the floor. A frown of concentration wrinkled the skin between her lovely eyes and she had sucked her lower lip into her mouth.

She didn't sense him in the room, so intently was she working at the task. As she turned so that her back was to him, he strode across the floor, grabbed her around the waist, and lifted her so he could nuzzle the skin at the back of her neck.

"Whoop... Ben." She wiggled about to throw her arms around his neck. "Lord, you scared me."

"Didn't mean to." He grinned down at her, and pushed a lock of hair from her face. Dear God, how he loved her. "Ah, Dessa. Come away with me. Be my love. Ride with me into the sunset, or some such nonsense. I love you, girl, what are we waiting for? Let's get married."

The outburst overwhelmed her, and she was temporarily speechless. Then she leaned back to get a good look at him.

"Well, of course you're right, Ben. We should just ride off into the sunset. Only, on what? You don't have a horse, and neither do I. We could steal Rose's blacks, perhaps. Neither of us has more than a stitch or two of clothes, we have no place to live but here, and you can see with the two of us in the room, elbows bump walls. But yes, Ben, let's throw caution to the wind and get married."

He squinted at her. "You're making fun of me."

She laughed, tousled his hair until he joined her. "Not making fun of you, Ben, just being practical. First things first." She grew very serious then. "And first thing with me, I think you know, is to find this Celia Cross and see if my brother really is still alive. I thought you understood how I feel about that."

"Wiley and I run across a fella telling about plans under way to build a railroad up north of here. It may be way in the future, but if we could get up there now, buy up some of those businesses that are struggling to stay alive, folks that would welcome cold hard cash, we'd be sitting pretty. Hell, we could start out feeding the crews that lay the rails and go from there."

"I know you're right, Ben. And I agree, but not until I find Mitchell. Then will be plenty of time for us. I promise. Just this one thing. You must understand, Ben. I love Mitchell, ever since he didn't come back from the war I've had this feeling about him, this sense of a connection. If it weren't for that, I would have died that night you found me. It was Mitchell, or my memory of him, that kept me going, kept me alive. Have you never loved someone that much, Ben?"

"Yes, I have. And I love you that much, too," Ben replied. "So let's get to looking for this Cross woman. Sooner she's found, sooner we can get on with it."

Dessa planted noisy kisses all over his face, hanging on to him so that he had to bend down. Both ended up laughing hilariously and he finally lifted her off the floor and straightened.

Arms firmly around her, he drew her close, their bodies welding together.

She looked up into his eyes, saw they had turned deep and dark as pools in a forest. A faint joyful purling, primitive in its rhythm, captured her, and she wanted only to have him deep inside her, probing, searching for her very soul. His presence became everything; there was nothing else. She let herself go, became his, became part of him.

He bent forward until his features were a blur. "Oh, God, Dessa, I need you," he said into her mouth.

He was fire, he was sweet, cool nourishment, and she drank, tasting the essence of this man. His desire rose against her, fierce and throbbing, and she shifted so that through her clothes she could feel that live, wonderful part of him pulsating at the heart of her own ravenous need. If he asked, she would give him what he wanted, what he must have, right here, this very minute.

"Dance with me," he said in a husky whisper. "Like this, up close." Then he began to sway, holding her so close she sensed every tenuous motion. A dizzying sensation of desire swelled within her and she moaned softly. He continued to move, breathing heavily against her neck, making tiny sounds down deep in his throat.

Arms wrapped tightly around his neck, she tasted of his flesh, whispered, "Love me, love me, love me."

"Oh, yes. Yes. Always and forever. Listen, my love. Hear the music?" He swept her around the room then in a graceful waltz, their bodies moving as one to the imaginary strains.

She heard the music, a melody from Liebestraum that welled as if from the most beautiful place imaginable.

His hot breath came in short puffs, stirring her hair. He groaned. "Oh, God, Dessa. I thank Clarice for one thing."

"Uhm, what is that?" she asked in a fuzzy voice, her tongue and lips thick with desire.

"She taught me how to dance. And I see the attraction, I surely do." He chuckled gruffly and lifted her feet off the floor, whirled her once, twice, three times, then let her go. Set her back from him.

"Whoo, that's enough of that."

She felt dizzy, disoriented, and staggered a couple of steps before righting herself. What would going to bed with this man be like when the simple act of dancing or holding each other could be so passionate, so physically disturbing?

"'I love you, girl, but stay where you are. I'm warning you." He turned quickly away, shoulders rising and falling as he took deep breaths and collected himself.

"And I love you, too, Ben. Oh, indeed I do."

Ben laughed self-consciously and turned back to her.

How wonderful that laughter was. He didn't enjoy life enough, and Dessa wished she could do something about that.

They parted reluctantly, the issue of her brother unsettled. She remained stubborn about finding him before they got on with their own lives, and he vowed to hold himself in check, not forcing his hungry needs on her before they were married.

Dessa stood in the doorway, waving to Ben. She watched the freight wagon out of sight. It was Friday, time for her to visit with Rose at the Golden Sun and ask her about Celia Cross.

Later that day she backed from her door, closing it and securing the hasp. As she turned, she spotted a familiar figure on horseback and froze in horror. He wasn't looking in her direction, and for that she was thankful. For Coody, the vicious outlaw who had dragged her off the stagecoach some two months ago, rode bold as brass right down the middle of the street.

"Just as if he were an ordinary person," Dessa muttered under her breath. Her heart thumped hard against her ribcage. Suppose he turned around, saw her? What would he do? What should she do?

She remained motionless in the doorway until he passed on by, then ran across the street. Something behind her attracted Coody's attention, the barking of a dog or someone shouting, and he swung around to look directly at her. She had no time to turn away. In that terrifying moment when their eyes met and locked, she knew he recognized her. And he wasn't going to let it go at that. He hunkered in the saddle and spurred the horse back in her direction.

Crying out, she scrambled up on the boardwalk and raced for the alley along one side of the Golden Sun. Dusk had fallen and the narrow opening lay in deep shadows. A side door that led into the back room where Grisham kept the whiskey stored might be unlocked, and if it was, she could sneak through there before Coody spotted her.

She hit the door with the flat of both hands and it popped open. With a heavy sigh, she slid inside and leaned against the wall until her breathing slowed and the fear that had boiled into her throat became a settled monster throbbing in her chest.

Then she ran through the storage room, intending on going into the saloon, where she would be safe. She ran right into Maggie, who had just stepped behind the bar.

"Dessa, whatever is wrong? You look awful."

"Hide me, Maggie. Hide me. It's him. I saw him. Right outside. He'll kill me. Hide me." Dessa panted and gasped out the words, squeezing Maggie's upper arm painfully.

"Who, Dessa? Where?" The girl waited, blocking their escape up the stairs and out of sight just long enough for Coody to burst through the saloon doors astride his sorrel horse. Patrons scattered in all directions, hugging walls and hitting the floor behind up-turned tables.

Maggie grabbed Dessa's arm and together they bolted for the stairway. It was too late. Dessa barely saw the reaction of the early evening patrons before Coody drew his pistol and started firing. She thought she saw Ben at the bar, and Rose behind it, down on the other end, but it was all a reddish blur in the half-light.

Women screamed, men shouted, shots rang out, and Maggie went down, her grip still tight on Dessa's arm, so that Dessa, too, was pulled down to sprawl on the staircase.

Ben scarcely had time to realize what was happening, and he watched with disbelief. His Winchester stood against the bar because he'd been on his way back from the short freight run with Wiley Moss. The rifle was loaded and he snatched it up, threw himself over and behind the bar to draw a bead on the man riding the terrified horse.

Sweat popped out on his forehead. He heard the screams of a thousand men dying on the battlefield, listened with disbelief to the echo of his vow that he would never put a bullet in another human being. He wiped sweat from his eyes with one arm, remembered Clete Woodridge's dying eyes beseeching his own murderer to take care of his wife and children. And he couldn't pull the trigger, he couldn't kill Coody.

Then the outlaw was gone, riding out the door and off the boardwalk, spurring his bucking horse, firing into the air as he rode hell-bent for leather out of Virginia City.

Ben lowered the rifle slowly, again wiped sweat from his eyes with his shirtsleeves, and gazed around the room. Upturned tables shielded men who had only recently been peacefully sipping beer or talking to their favorite dancing partner. A couple of girls peered wild-eyed from behind the staircase.

Then someone started screaming, and the screams grew in intensity until they split the air and set his nerves on end.

He located the screams beyond the solid railing of the stairs. He vaulted over the bar. Dear God, it was Dessa screaming. She was holding Maggie in her arms and both were covered with blood. They might have been bathing in it. And Dessa just kept right on screaming and rocking the limp body back and forth.

For the longest moment in his life, Ben couldn't move. Then he leaped up the stairs and knelt with his arms wrapped around the women he loved, one alive, the other dead.

Eight

Ben's thoughts, his very existence clouded as he roughly embraced the two women. A blackness washed over him, driving all sanity into the farthest and darkest corners of his consciousness. Rose knelt beside him, but he was barely aware of her. He could only stare into the dead face of dear, sweet Maggie, who had literally dragged him back from the depths of despair when he was no more than a child. He couldn't speak or cry out; he thought he could not draw a breath. He prayed his own heart would just stop beating and solve everything. He'd had Maggie's killer in his sights and couldn't pull the trigger.

Rose lay her hand on his arm. Dessa stopped screaming and began to cry in jerking sobs, her face buried in his shoulder. She repeated Maggie's name over and over and over like a litany that might somehow restore life. When Ben didn't respond to her touch, Rose lay her hand on Dessa's head and just sat there on the step, staring sightlessly.

Dear Maggie was dead, and Rose's tough exterior fell away as if someone were chopping at her with an ax. But she had to minister to the living, these two young people whom she loved with all her heart and soul.

From deep in Ben's throat there rose a roar of agony that turned every head in the room. He lay Maggie gently down, pulled away from Dessa, and rose from where he knelt, still making the awful noise that those in the saloon that night would speak of in awe for years afterward. He staggered to the bar, retrieved the Winchester from where he'd thrown it, and burst out the door. His wounded cry could be heard echoing into the distance long after the doors stopped swinging. Still no one in the Golden Sun moved. It was as if they'd been stricken mute and turned to stone.

Dessa's trembling query broke the silence. "Rose?"

"I don't know, child, I just don't know."

"Where is he going?"

"To kill that monster, I would think. And if and when he does that, he might as well shoot himself."

"What do you mean?"

"I mean if Ben Poole causes one more death, he will not be able to live with it. I saw him the last time. If you love him and you think you can stop him, child, please go after him. If you don't, we'll all lose him forever."

"That awful man deserves to die, Rose. He killed Maggie. He came after me and he killed Maggie. Oh, Rose, my God," she wailed. "I... I came... He was after me, and I came in here. She was helping me get away. Oh, Rose."

"Sshh, sweetheart. You mustn't blame yourself. It was him that caused it all, from beginning to end. That brutish Coody Land. And yes, he does deserve to die, but Ben doesn't deserve to be the one who kills him. Let someone else blow the son of a bitch away. Let it not be Ben. Pray it's not Ben. I'm going to fetch Walter Moohn. If you love that man, go after him, right now. Take one of my horses. Quick, go!"

Rose lifted her skirts from the gore and ran down the stairs, her own blood running as cold as the snowmelt off the mountains. Shock would not yet allow her to cry for the death of sweet, sweet Maggie, who had been like a daughter to her for so many years. Later, much later she could wail and tear her hair. Now she had to do what she always did: take care of things. It was her purpose in this life. There was Samuel to notify. He had gone back to Nebraska to make ready for his new wife... Maggie, his new wife. Rose's breath caught in a huge sob.

Don't think. Just keep moving. Keep moving. Outside the batwing doors she stumbled into the arms of a pale-faced Walter Moohn.

"Holy thunderation, Rose. What happened in there?" the sheriff asked, holding the trembling woman close to his chest.

Behind them Dessa ran onto the boardwalk, eyes wildly searching up and down the street.

"Where did Ben go? Did you see him? Which way did he go?"

"Rode that way," Moohn said, and pointed in the direction opposite from the livery. "I hollered, but he didn't pay me no mind. Now will someone tell me what went on over here? All the uproar sounded like war had done broke out."

Rose pulled him inside and glanced once over her shoulder in the direction Dessa had gone. Down toward the livery and a mount.

"Oh, dear God, let them both come back safe," she said aloud, then turned to the matter at hand. The poor, bloody dead woman sprawled on the stairs. Most of the rest of the girls were nearly hysterical. Everyone loved Maggie. What would they all do without her pixie face, her cheerful laughter, her caring heart?

Blinded by tears, Dessa fingered a bit into Baron's mouth, slipped the bridle up and over his ears, and crawled on his back. No time for a saddle. Ben had taken Beauty, the faster of the two blacks, and she might never catch him, but she had to try. She had led the evil Coody Land into that saloon, no matter how Rose might rationalize it, and she would not allow Ben Poole to kill because of her.

He would never forgive himself. He would never smile again and those blue eyes would frost over forever.

Dessa hunkered low against the gelding's neck and urged him on, past the sheriff's office and beyond the straggle of empty miner's shacks on the outskirts of town, up the slope past Boot Hill and into the face of the rising full moon. The horse's hooves hammered along the trail. She prayed the two men had not cut cross-country, for she might never find them. But she had to try. Dear Lord, she had to try. The huge golden moon swelled into the darkened sky to light the way. The trail grew more treacherous and she was forced to slow down or she would tumble head over heels into the ravine far below.

The gelding blew and snorted as he trotted, sweat lathered his hide, stiff hairs chafed her skin through the thin cotton pantaloons. She thought she heard the soft whinny of another horse and drew up to listen. In the ebony stillness rocks clattered from somewhere high above and off to her left, and she craned her neck, staring in that direction. Another scattering of loose gravel, and then all was quiet. Shadows probed the night, hung around her like hungry ghosts waiting to pounce.

Someone or something was up there, hiding and watching. But who? Land or Ben? And if only one of them, where was the other? The distant whinny came again from up ahead, and she urged Baron forward, toward the chatter of rushing water. She spotted a vague trail heading downward off to the right.

The gelding whickered and an answer came back from the shadows where patches of moonlight played tag. She reined him down the trail, riding slowly, ears tingling with an overpowering silence. If Land lay in wait, she was lost. But if it was Ben... oh, please let it be Ben.

She and her mount broke through the canopy of thick foliage into a small clearing along the bank of a roiling creek that shone silver in the moonlight. And standing there, head thrown back and arms spread, was Ben Poole, golden hair glowing like foxfire.

Dessa slid off Baron's back and left him rubbing noses with Beauty. She didn't know what to say or do. A relief grew within her, so exquisite, so overpowering that all she could do was reach out to him, feel his aliveness and soothe his soul. Gently she lay one hand on his back. Under her fingers muscles quivered and twitched; otherwise he didn't move or say anything. His flesh burned. She could feel the heat emanating through the sweat soaked shirt.

"Ben?" she crooned, and reached to entwine the fingers of her other hand into his upraised one.

He sucked in a deep, jagged breath.

"Oh, Ben," she said, and moved around him, tucking herself up against the statue of stone he appeared to be.

"She's dead," he whispered in a voice dry as husks.

"I'm sorry." She breathed the words against his chest as if in doing so she could bring him back to life. How much had he loved Maggie, to grieve like this? She ached with an envy that came and went. She loved Ben that much and more; she had to help him.

Without warning, he wrapped both arms around her, cradling the back of her head with one large hand and burying his face in the curve of her shoulder. "Oh, God, oh, God. Why didn't I kill him?"

He stood hunched over her, swaying, and she feared she would collapse under the weight of his sorrow.

Finally, after what seemed an eternity, he stirred and kissed her ear, her neck, her throat.

Her pent-up grief exploded in a moan and she turned to meet his searching lips with her own.

"Hold me, love me," she cried, as if somehow she could steal him away from the spirit of sorrow. At last she understood his love for Maggie, for she saw in him the same agony she had experienced when they told her Mitchell was dead.

"Oh, Ben, my love. I know. I do know."

He clung to her, seeking her love, her warmth, her compassion. She was alive and sweet and caring. Her breasts rose and fell and he lowered his head to their lushness.

"I love you, Dessa. Don't leave me, I love you." Fingers fumbling along the swell of her flesh, he unhooked the fabric of her dress, then tore at the shift, his need a pulsing, living thing. Mouth at her bared breast, he groaned and cried out, like a baby starving for nourishment.

The wild wet caress of his tongue and teeth and lips ignited the smoldering desire she had so carefully kept under control, fanned the coals so they burst to life and roared within her. She arched her back, gave him first one breast, then the other.

He fed there, the sweetness of his kisses mixing with the heat of his tears on her flesh. The ecstasy of giving him sustenance, his taking it with such frenzy, awoke in her a fever of lust. She vibrated with it, blind to everything but her passion.

If she could have crawled inside him, felt his heart flutter, touched the trail of his thoughts, she would have. He caught her up in his arms and went to his knees in the crackle of last year's leaves and drying grasses. Long legs astraddle her, he loosened the opening of her skirt, tugged it free of her hips along with the slips and underthings.

In the cold air, goose bumps rippled across her stomach and she was overcome with an intense desire to touch his bare skin, to see it and feel it and kiss it. She reached a trembling hand to the waist of his jeans and when she touched him, he sucked in his breath. He put his hand over hers and slid it downward until she cupped the throbbing center of his desire.

Until that moment their lovemaking had been a frantic denial of death, a human celebration that, despite what had happened, they were still alive. Now Dessa felt him calm down, rein in his passion so that they paused on the brink of desire. From the mo-ment he had begun this primitive ritual, she had gone along with him, moved with him, and grown heavy with a deep need to complete the act no matter the consequences.

Now he let her decide. He held her hand on his manhood an instant longer, then took away his own and gazed down at her, the blue of his eyes glittering like ice in the moonlight.

Slowly, never taking her eyes from his, she began to unfasten the buttons down the front of his pants.

Ben rocked backward and tilted his head until he was looking up into the moonglow against the purple velvet sky. The cool caress of her hands as she pulled the jeans down over his hips soothed the heated agony in his soul. His desire became a palpable thing, something he could actually touch with the fingers of his mind.

Maggie was dead and it seemed no disrespect to her memory to take this woman, whom he loved with all his being, for his own true spiritual mate.

Her hands cupped his buttocks and he leaned forward, settling into the dark nest between her legs. Probing there, searching for the sweet well.

In a pool of golden light he saw she had her eyes closed, as if frightened, her arms thrown above her head in submission.

"Dessa?"

"Oh, Ben. Yes, please, now." She lifted her hips so that he was pressed tightly against her.

A wild, wonderful feeling came over him, as if moonlight had turned to warm liquid gold to spread over them, encasing their bodies forever in a statue of love. He entered her with a deep-throated moan. She answered in kind, cried out sharply once, twice, when he broke her maidenhead. Then they were together moving as one. Flowing beyond the singing water, above the softly swaying trees, riding beams of moonlight into the purple darkness of space. Shards of stars crackled around them, like ice, like fire, like the promise of eternity. They moved on. Together. Forever.

He thought he might have lain there always, had she not turned so that he no longer felt her body coiled against his.

"Dessa?"

"Yes, Ben. Oh, yes."

"Did I hurt you?"

"No…well, only for an instant, but then it was fine. Very, very fine."

He turned, propped himself on an elbow. She lay on her back, her skirt kicked off into a pile at her feet. Cold air danced all around them, laden with a rising mist from the water. He reached a tentative finger and touched the erect bud of her breast.

"Cold," she said, and lay her palm alongside his face.

He closed his eyes. "Don't be sorry. I'm not."

"Sorry? I'm not sorry. Why would I be?"

"Well, like maybe it was disrespectful, with Maggie dying and all, that we finally… well, made love."

"It was love. It was that. Yours. Hers. Mine. Ours."

Ben gazed fondly at her. 'Yes, it was. It is. I remember the feeling... It's like in the war. Bodies lying everywhere, men you loved, fought with, should have died with. Death brings it on, a feeling hard to describe. You feel guilty you're alive and they're dead, but you can't help but thank God for letting you live. And you feel suddenly more alive than ever before."

She breathed softly for a while, said nothing.

He went on, his voice so muffled she could barely hear it above the rushing water. "I thank God you're alive. What if he had killed you, too? When I saw all that blood, I thought he had." His voice choked, and he closed his eyes momentarily.

She experienced a quiver of regret, pleasure, relief? She wasn't sure. Ben was right, there was no describing it.

Beyond his shoulder hung the depths of the night sky. How good it was to be lying here in his arms. How exquisite to feel his body against hers. A deep swell of contentment filled her.

"Do you think she... Maggie... would mind?" he asked, his voice breaking once again and tears gleaming.

"Did you love her truly?"

He nodded. "She was my anchor, she was my sister. She saved my life, and I don't know what I'll do without her."

"Your sweet sister," Dessa whispered. She rubbed a thumb over her full lower lip. "I know... like Mitchell."

He nibbled at her thumb. "I wanted to kill him for what he did to her... to you. I came out here to do that, but in the end I watched him ride away from me and didn't take my shot. I could have put a bullet right between his shoulder blades and I didn't."

"Oh, thank God you didn't, Ben. Maggie wouldn't have wanted you to do that."

"What, shoot the man who killed her?" His voice was disdainful, unbelieving.

"No, ruin your life for her. If it had been me, Ben, me he killed, I know I would never want you to ruin your life to avenge my death. Rose said…she said that you…that you… once, you told me you had killed someone. Once, a long time ago when we were still trying to find reasons we shouldn't fall in love. And tonight when Rose sent me after you, she said that if you killed again, I would lose you forever. We would all lose you forever."

"Maybe so. I don't know. It's a weakness in me, I guess. I saw so much killing when I was so young. My mother, my sisters, slaughtered and raped before my eyes when I was only thirteen. Men blown to bloody bits all around me during the war when I wasn't much older. I made a vow—I pledged never to kill again. Never to have anything to do with death."

"And then I… there was a robbery in town." He paused, shuddered.

She put her arms around him. Head resting in the crook of his shoulder, she listened in silence, grateful that at last he would tell her.

"The bank. I was in town, walking down from the freight station carrying my rifle, when three of 'em busted out the doors shooting at anything that moved. They killed Mrs. Drew and her young'un, just shot them down in the middle of the street.

"I fell to my belly, rolled behind a horse trough, and when one of 'em started to mount and ride away, I came up shooting." Ben gulped audibly, rubbed harshly at her skin with his thumb.

"I didn't see Clete. He ran out from around the other side of the livery. One of my bullets caught him in the chest, must've got his heart. But he… but he lived long enough to look into my eyes. I swear, Dessa, he never knew it was me who shot him, but I've always been afraid he did. Oh, God, suppose he knew."

"Oh, Ben, no. How could he? For that matter, how could you? Bullets flying everywhere. Where was the sheriff, other men in town? All of you shooting, I'd bet. Why, even one of the outlaws could have shot him."

"Ben, is that why you and Sarah Woodridge…was Clete her husband?"

He nodded. "Last thing he said to me was, 'See to my wife and babies. Promise you'll see to them.'"

"And so you promised."

He nodded. "I didn't want to talk about this now, after we've been together. Ah, Lord, Dessa. You are a wonder. I've never felt such a thing as we had tonight."

She smiled. "Neither have I, Ben, neither have I."

He shivered and hugged her up close. "It's freezing out here. Let's get back."

They dressed quickly, self-conscious in a way that surprised Ben. They had, after all, been together as man and wife. He hoped soon to make that a reality.

It was deep in the night when Dessa and Ben quietly led their mounts into the livery and darted through the darkest shadows of a sleeping Virginia City, sneaked into her small house, and fell exhausted into bed.

They didn't learn until the next day that Walter Moohn and a quickly organized posse had left at sunup to track the outlaw Coody Land. They had followed his trail into the foothills of Alder Gulch where, as time and time before, they lost it on the hardscrabble rocks.

They sat in the Golden Sun early the next evening, Rose and Walter Moohn, Ben and Dessa, trying to make sense out of the horrible killing. Maggie's funeral, held that afternoon at Boot Hill, had brought out many of the men in town. Men, that is, who weren't married.

Rose laughed bitterly. "The rest would have come, too, if they dared. Maggie had a way of making any man feel like he was the best there was. But they daren't be seen at the funeral of a whore. Ah, my poor, poor Maggie. And poor Samuel. I shudder to think what he'll do when he gets my wire."

Moohn squeezed Rose's hand and didn't say anything until the mood passed. Then he said, changing the subject, "Yank and his gang are hid out in Alder Gulch. Ain't no posse gonna ride in there to get bushwhacked. There just ain't enough law in Montana Territory to face down such a gang of cutthroats and owlhoots."

"What's wrong with the army?" Ben asked, sipping at his cold beer and holding tightly to Dessa's hand under the table.

"They're too busy protecting the railroads and riding herd on Sitting Bull to worry too much about outlaws yahooing a town like Virginia City. We could catch Land out and away from Yank's bunch, we'd take care of him."

"We?" Dessa asked.

"I'll deputize some townfolk. It's all we've got," Moohn said.

"What would you do to him?" Dessa said in a small voice.

"Same thing we done to Joseph Slade. He wouldn't leave the town alone. Got to where ever damn Saturday night he'd ride his horse right into the Busted Mule or Sadie's—Rose wasn't here then—and just shoot up everthing. Killed a few folks, too. We just got plumb fed up with it. Finally run him down one evening, hung the son of a bitch from a corral post. His wife pounding her poor old bony chest and pleading for his life. But when you've had enough, why, then you've just had enough. There weren't any sympathy left, not even for his pitiful wife."

Rose nodded. "Well, as far as I'm concerned, the time has come I've had enough of that Coody Land, so I hope you're set to stretch his neck the very next time he comes yahooing this town."

"You know I ain't never been a gunhand. Folks just grabbed me up to serve as lawman 'cause I was handy. Hell, they ain't no law in the territories but what we can make ourselves. Best we can do is wait for that bunch to try something, and this time we'll be ready. We'll either hang 'em or shoot 'em down, and there won't be anyone crying over it either.

"Sometimes, Rose, I wish I was anything but sheriff. It just don't suit me too much. I reckon I just never took to the job."

She covered his hands with her own and didn't say anything.

Ben remained content to listen to the conversation. He had done his best to put away his sorrow over Maggie's death. It was time he and Dessa made some plans. There was nothing for it but to find Celia Cross and learn just what she knew about Mitchell Fallon. Because until they did, Dessa wouldn't even consider talking about their own future. And then, of course, there was the one chore he'd put off too long. There was Sarah to deal with, and he had to face the fact that she loved him. It would hurt her some, but he knew now that it had to be.

Not being one to let things lie too long, Molly Blair picked later that very evening to launch yet another attack with her hoe-, shovel-, and broom-wielding army. On Saturday the saloons and the hurdy-gurdy house were crammed to overflowing. The unholy brigade hit the Busted Mule first, for gamblers seemed to gather at an earlier hour than did those who wanted the company of a fair young woman.

By the time the ladies reached the Golden Sun, word had spread around town that the preacher's wife was on the rampage. Rose was in a fury. How dare that bunch do such a thing, with poor Maggie not cold in the ground? The least they could have done was have a little decency and give everyone time to mourn.

So it was with fire in her eye that the owner of the Golden Sun marched out on the boardwalk to face down her detractors. And she carried the shotgun Grisham kept tucked behind the bar. The one he never got a chance to use on Coody Land.

Before Molly Blair could open her mouth, Rose hugged the stock into her shoulder, aimed the twelve-gauge over the heads of the crowd, and pulled the trigger. The kick knocked her backward into the wall of the saloon. She sprung forward, set her feet wide apart, jacked another round in, and raised the weapon again.

The stampeding herd of women halted fast and milled about like confused cattle, looking to Molly to make the next move.

Rose never took the gun from her shoulder. "That's all the warning you're getting, you church-house mice. I'm going to count to three and if you ain't showing me the tails of your skirts by then, I'm gonna blast a hole right in the middle of the bunch of you. Who catches buckshot catches buckshot, and that's all there is to it."

About that time, fresh from the altercation at the Busted Mule—which had taken a while to settle after the women left—Sheriff Walter Moohn came striding along the boardwalk, spurs jingling and bootheels thunking hard like he meant business.

The tone of his voice proved he did. "Now, hold it just a minute. I've had me about enough of law-breaking for a while. You ladies git on back home where you belong, and Rose, you put that hogleg down before you do something you'll regret."

"I won't regret filling any one of these old heifers with buckshot, Walter Moohn. And I'll thank you kindly to just butt out."

Moohn drew up and gaped at Rose. "Butt out? Rose, I'm the dang-blamed sheriff."

"Lot of good that does me. I'm gonna pick me out one and shoot." She swung the barrel around, drawing bead on first one, then another of the frightened women who looked like they wanted to run but were waiting for Molly to give the word.

Moohn dove for Rose, knocking the business end of the shotgun skyward just as it went off. Rose staggered into a post in front of the Golden Sun.

Moohn drew out his own gun, a long-barreled Colt .45 that he'd once bragged he used to take a potshot at Jessie James. No one knew if that was the truth. Moohn himself wasn't sure anymore, he'd told the story so many times.

"Now, ladies. I'm not the kind of man to lose my temper with the fair sex—"

An audible sigh went up from the church ladies at the mention of such a word as sex, in any connotation.

"But I've just about had my fill of all of you. Now, Miss Rose, you can't go shooting people just 'cause they're gathered in a public street. And Mrs. Blair, you can't take it upon yourself to close down a place of business just 'cause you don't approve of what goes on behind the doors.

"So I'm giving you all fair warning. I've had you all in jail once, and I ain't agin putting you all there again. Now, disperse, the lot of you, or I'll start rounding you up. And this time no husband is going to appear to drag you off home. You'll stay till I say you can leave."

He held the Colt down along his thigh and glared hard at everyone. Then in a booming voice that caused horses down the street to whinny in fright, he shouted, "Move it, now!" He turned and tipped his hat to a wide-eyed Rose. "And you'll excuse me, Miss Rose, but that means you, too. Inside, now."

Nearly an hour later, Walter Moohn strolled down a peaceful Saturday night street in his town of Virginia City, turned sharply to his left at the batwing doors of the Golden Sun, and went inside. He ordered a beer at the bar and carried it to the table at which Rose Langue sat scowling and nursing her own mug of brew.

He got himself situated, being careful that he didn't jar the table, then looked squarely at the beautiful saloon owner and said, "I want you to marry me, soon as we can arrange it, and come away with me out West."

A tight-lipped, angry Rose stared hotly at her suitor. "Not in a million years, Walter Moohn. Not in a million years. Now get your butt out of my saloon, and don't you come back."

She took a deep breath and rose, expanding her awesome breasts to their fullest. "And I don't want you to look at me or speak to me. I want you to even cross the street when you see me coming."

"Aw, Rose, don't get all ornery on me. I was doing my job."

"Your job? I've never been so humiliated in my life. Manhandling me like I'm a common whore.

"I'm leaving this town, all right, but not with you. I'm going somewhere where folks appreciate a place where they can relax and have a good time. This is a decent place, and I don't have to put up with the likes of that oh-so-snooty, sermon-spouting Molly Blair. Just who does she think she is? And dear Maggie not even cold in the ground."

Rose began to cry then, and whirled away, hoping Moohn wouldn't see the tears. She'd not have him thinking her weakening in her resolve.

Walter felt bad about the entire episode, but he couldn't think how he could have handled it any other way. He'd kept everyone from getting hurt, hadn't he? And that was what he was there for. He stood in the middle of the floor and watched Rose climb the stairs to her private rooms. Then, when she was gone, the door upstairs slammed firmly behind her, he crammed his grimy hat down tight on his head and stalked out of the Golden Sun.

Maybe she'd be in a better mood the next day and he could try again. He had no intention of giving up his attempt to marry Rose Langue. She was the most beautiful woman he'd ever seen, and while he had no notion what she might accidentally see in him, she had taken a liking to him and let him know it. He wasn't a man to give up easily.

Second on his agenda that night was a surprise for the next owlhoot who rode into his town, and he headed down toward the livery, where a few trusted men waited. There was no sense in putting this off.

Nine

The issue of his debt to Sarah Woodridge rested heavily on Ben's shoulders, and so he rode out Sunday morning while Dessa attended church. She wanted to pray for Maggie, she said, and he nodded. He would pray on the creek bank or out beneath the tall pines. Besides, it was time he straightened out this problem with Sarah. It had already gone on too long.

The nearer he came to the Woodridge place, the slower he rode. Oh, how he dreaded facing her. She loved him, and he cared for her and her boys, but it wasn't the same as love. Not the same as the way he felt about Dessa. Guilt was not a proper companion for two people starting a new life.

The Woodridge home was almighty quiet when he rode into the yard. It was a blustery day, and he knew she hadn't set foot in church since Clete died, so she and the boys must be inside. Where would she go?

The twins heard his steps on the porch. Shouting madly, they burst out the doorway and hurled themselves around his legs. He hobbled stiffly inside, dragging the laughing boys along.

Sarah stood in the center of the room, a humpbacked wooden

trunk open beside her. She held something in her hand that could have been a bedsheet or a tablecloth, he couldn't tell.

"Ben," she said, and her eyes filled with tears. "Oh, I'm so glad you came. Where have you been so long?"

Clearly she knew, for everyone in town was aware that Ben Poole had accompanied Dessa Fallon to Kansas City. She would be no exception, despite the remote locale of her farm.

He dragged the two youngsters along with him as he crossed the room and planted a kiss on her forehead. She leaned up against him for a moment, then pulled away.

"What're you doing?" He hefted the squirming boys, one on each arm. They giggled and pulled at his hat. "Look out there, tadpoles, you'll rip my best hat in two if you aren't careful."

Sarah offered a weak smile. "Packing. I'm packing."

"I can see that, but what for?"

She dropped the cloth. "Let me get you some coffee. Boys, git on in the other room and finish your jobs. Mama wants to talk to Ben. Git, now, go on."

The boys obeyed when Ben fanned playfully at their backsides with his hat.

Sarah waited until she had poured coffee and they were both seated at the table. She ran a finger around the rim of her cup, then raised her eyes to him. "I'm leaving, going back to Philadelphia. It's Clete's folks. They want to see the kids, want to watch them grow up. Say they've lost their son, it's only fair they have a replacement. I... oh, Ben, I...." Tears flowed freely down her cheeks.

He gazed down at the table. "Sarah, I'm so sorry. God, I'm sorry. For... for everything." He gestured wide, taking in the room, the whole outside, the world.

She nodded. "You can't go on being sorry all your life, though. It ain't fair. Not to you nor me nor... nor Clete. It happened. It just happened, and Lord knows we've all paid dearly. It's enough." She waited a moment, picking at a thread in her apron. "You love her, don't you?"

He nodded his head.

"She's real pretty, a sweet little thing, from what I could see. Oh, Ben, I wish you well. I truly do. And I thank you for what you've done for us, me and the boys. The other, well, it just couldn't be helped, and you hadn't ought to go on blaming yourself anymore."

They were both quiet for a long while, listening to the boys bickering softly in the other room.

He cleared his throat. "When will you leave?"

"Midweek. They sent me money to ship our things. I'll be hiring a freighter to take them down to the train station in Devil's Gate."

"Bannon's a fine line," Ben chided, trying to lighten the mood of the moment. There were other freighters in town, and he wasn't even sure he'd be making any more runs with Wiley Moss. It depended on what he and Dessa decided to do.

As if reading his mind, Sarah asked, "Will you marry soon?"

"I think so, as soon as a few things are settled."

"Well, Ben, don't wait too long. Time can sometimes be short, and we need to go on with things fast as we can."

"Yeah, well, we will."

'Tell her I said... tell her I said she's getting the best man in Virginia City and she'd better treat him right."

Ben rose as Sarah did and gave her a brief hug. "You take care of those boys, and yourself, too."

"Oh, I will. Now, go on, git out of here. I've got work to do."

Ben didn't look back as he left Woodridge farm behind, but kept his eyes on the trail ahead.

It seemed as if the small town of Virginia City was

doomed, for soon after Sunday midnight, Coody Land and his sidekick paid another visit.

Ben was asleep in the hay of the livery. He was trying to work himself up to sleeping in a bed by stretching out in the loose hay. He figured he was coming ever closer to being comfortable on a civilized mattress. Dessa and he had said goodnight hours before after an evening of discussing her riding off into Alder Gulch on her own to try to find her brother. It had been a bitter argument, but they had parted warmly. Ben figured it wouldn't be much longer before he'd have to tie her to the bed to keep her from heading out on her own.

Satisfied he had convinced her sufficiently to keep her from running off that very night, he was sleeping deeply when the gunfire erupted. It sounded like a war breaking out. He hopped into his britches on one foot, then the other in the middle of the barn before he realized where he was or what he was doing.

As he raced out into the street, he heard breaking glass, the pounding of hooves, and the staccato sound of more rapid gunshots. Two men on horseback came right at him, firing randomly. He scurried for cover inside the livery. Damn! Why hadn't he grabbed his Winchester? It lay back there in the darkness beside his bed of hay. Before he could hunt for the rifle, a bevy of mounted men thundered by, hot on the heels of the vanishing outlaws.

Ben ran out again. What the hell was going on?

Sheriff Moohn slowed his prancing Appaloosa and shouted at him. "Mount up, we're gonna get those sons a bitches this time if we have to chase 'em clear to California."

Ben was dumbstruck. The sheriff had been ready and waiting. What was wrong with that fool Land? What was he after, or who? After shooting Maggie, he'd gotten away free and clear, only to turn around and come back now. Ben wasted no more time. He was going with the posse, for he couldn't wait here while they avenged dear Maggie's death. He had to have a hand in it, even if he didn't pull the trigger on the man. He might have a cowardly weakness for outright killing, but he had no aversion to assisting in carrying out justice.

Lamps were lit in windows all over town as the men rode out. Ben followed along on Rose's black gelding, his Winchester in its scabbard at his knee.

The posse galloped past Dessa's. Scared awake by the earlier noise, she peered through her window holding a lamp high in one hand. Ben spotted her pale, wide-eyed face in a blur, not sure if she saw him. He didn't wave or slow. Just like Moohn and the rest of the town, he'd had enough of Coody Land. If they caught the outlaws this night, Ben knew he would do what had to be done, along with the others. It was distasteful, this vigilante business, but there was nothing else for it. Men would break the law, and until some kind of law enforcement agencies were formed, ordinary men like Moohn had to pin on a badge and hope to keep some semblance of peace.

Land had tried to kill Dessa and, worse, would have if she hadn't escaped; he had succeeded in killing poor old J.T. and Artie and then dear Maggie. It was time he paid for his crimes. Justice would be meted out in the only way Walter Moohn and every man-jack in that posse knew. Ben wanted to be there for it. He wanted to make up for not shooting that coward Land in the back when he had the chance.

A combination of luck and the sly planning of Sheriff Moohn brought about the capture of Coody Land and his young sidekick. Justice would at last come down on the two men who had brutally murdered the stage driver and his guard, then dragged Dessa off the stagecoach and sent her wandering into the arms of the man she now loved.

Land and the younger outlaw, known only as the kid, obviously assured they had gotten away clean, lay in a stand of pine not ten miles from town sharing a jug of whiskey they'd stolen from the Busted Mule.

"Nothin' like a good hurrah to get yore blood to the boiling point," the kid remarked to Land, then poured more fiery liquid down his throat.

"Danged idjit. I wanted the gal. What'd you have to go and start shootin' for?"

"Sheiit, fool. How'd you think you would find her?"

Land slobbered all around the neck of the bottle drunkenly, finally managed to upend it and slosh whiskey into his mouth. Wetly, he mumbled, "Take her to that sumbitch Yank, show him whose boss. Ignerant jackass. He don't quit shoving this ole boy around, I'm a gonna shoot him and be done with it."

The lad snickered. "You and what army? Lucky you didn't find the gal. Touch a man's sister, he'll do worse than just shoot you."

Riding at the head of the posse, Moohn spotted a saddled mount and called the boys to a halt, signaling silence. He slid to the ground and took up the dangling reins of a pair of meandering horses. Tying them to the nearest tree, he made a motion to the others to dismount.

It then became a simple matter of following the noise of the drunken argument, surrounding the men, and drawing their guns. There wasn't even a fight.

"Hang 'em right here," one of the posse members said, and holstered his pistol. "I got a rope. Alls we need is another'n."

"We'll have none a that," Moohn cautioned. "We'll take 'em back to town and hang 'em proper. That's what we got Hanging Gulch for. We'll let the whole town watch, then we can bury 'em right handily in Boot Hill. It'll be the end to another of our problems.

"Come on, Ben. Help me tie these ornery cusses to their horses. Blamed fools. Makes a feller wonder why they're either one still alive, stupid as they are."

"Hey, don't call me stupid," Land shouted, and passed out flat on his face in the pine needles.

The posse rode back into town against a dawn-silvered eastern sky, Land and the kid draped belly down over their saddles, ropes securing their feet to their wrists.

They hung the two outlaws bright and early that same morning. There was no question they were guilty—everyone in the Golden Sun had seen Land gun down Maggie. It was justice, pure and simple.

Dessa went to the hanging, as did everyone else in town, but she turned away at the last moment, when the two horses were slapped into bolting from beneath their riders. She would never forget the sounds of that violent event, though, the thick, guttural babbling, the cut-off moans, the creaking as the bodies twisted back and forth beneath the heavy limb of the hanging tree... the joyful shout that went up from the crowd, a baby crying in the stunned silence that followed.

"There, Maggie, there," she murmured, and tears flowed once more.

Ben took her arm and walked her away. Behind them the sharp chinking sound of shovels as two men finished digging the graves. She raised her eyes to look at the intense blue of the Montana sky. Far off to the northwest a bank of dark clouds gathered, boiling higher and higher as she watched. A gust of wind caught the hem of her skirts and in it she felt the kiss of approaching winter. It had already arrived in high country. Every morning the pristine peaks gleamed with new-fallen snow. Soon it would move down the mountains. She had only heard of the brutality of winter here in Montana Territory. A shiver of anticipation ran through her. Her and Ben in front of a fire, wrapped in quilts and each other's arms. But there was one bit of unfinished business to attend to before she dared let herself dream of such a wonder as that.

"I have to find Celia Cross, Ben. I have to find her now," she said, and her tone brooked no further nonsense. She had waited as long as she could.

He would have to give in and go with her, or she would go alone. No matter how closely he watched her, one day she would ride out in search of her brother.

"Have you asked Rose?"

"She doesn't know a Celia Cross. She said that she probably belongs to one of the outlaws living out at Alder Gulch. That's where Mitchell is, Ben. I just know it. Otherwise, someone in town would know him or remember seeing him."

"You think he's an outlaw?" Ben hurried her along the steep incline back to town. A cold wind whipped at his back like dread.

"A lot of men who survive war end up on the wrong side of the law, for one reason or another. He's in danger, Ben. We've got to find him."

"I'll ask around. Might be someone coming through and stopping at the Mule or at Rose's will know something about him. Then we'll see."

"I don't want to wait."

They were at her door now, and looking up, Ben saw Wiley Moss striding toward them, a purposeful glint in his eyes. "Uh-oh, looks as if I'm going to have to go to work."

"Oh, Ben."

"Promise me you won't do anything till I get back, Dessa. I'll go with you, but you have to wait. You could get yourself killed going out there alone."

"Mitchell wouldn't let anything happen to me."

"You don't know that he's out there. Please, don't be foolish. Promise me. This could just be a trick. Why hasn't the woman gotten in touch with you since your parents' death? I think she was trying to trick them into giving her some money, then she was just going to disappear."

Dessa secretly thought Ben might be right, but she hoped fervently that he wasn't. She couldn't bear to think it was all a lie, not after getting up her hopes.

Ben leaned down to kiss her, and Wiley averted his gaze, looking embarrassed.

"I just know he's alive, Ben," Dessa whispered, and opened the door.

He touched her cheek. "Okay, we'll find him together."

"When will you be back?"

Ben glanced at Wiley.

"Three Forks," the old driver said.

"Late tomorrow," Ben told her.

She nodded, then grabbed him around the neck and held on tightly. "Be careful," she said into his ear.

He shivered from the heat of her breath and hugged her close. "I love you."

She let him go and backed into the open doorway. She wouldn't say she loved him in front of Wiley, but she let her eyes tell him so before closing the door.

Rose came to visit the next day and the two women had dinner together at the Montana House, a welcome, down-to-earth change from the civilized cuisine of the Continental. Rose spoke of when Maggie had first come to the Golden Sun, reminiscing in a soft, faraway voice. Then she grew silent and Dessa didn't know what to say, so they finished their meal without speaking.

"Walter asked me to marry him. Again." Rose blurted.

"Oh, Rose. That's wonderful."

"Would be if he hadn't gone about it in such an all-fired typical manlike way."

Dessa couldn't stop a laugh. "Well, Rose, what did you expect? He is a man, after all."

Rose joined her merriment. "I guess you're right there."

"Are you going to?"

Rose picked at her apple pie with the tines of her fork. "I think so, but I'm not going to tell him for a while. Let him stew in his own juices, the old fart."

"Rose, shame on you."

"What about you and Ben?"

Dessa leaned back and gazed past Rose into the distance. "I love him."

"Well, of course you do, having good sense and all. He's the finest man a woman could want."

"Rose, you always were biased where Ben was concerned."

Rose sipped at her tea. "What will you do?"

"Do?" Dessa widened her eyes.

"You and Ben. What do you plan to do after you marry?"

"Oh, that. Well, first we have to see a good lawyer and get my father's will straightened out. That's a long story. Then Ben wants to go up north, says they're going to be building new railroads up there. We can invest in businesses, build up my father's holdings. Did you know Ben is brilliant with figures? I couldn't cipher my way out of a paper sack, and he just thinks it all out in his head, without even using a pencil or paper."

Rose laughed heartily. "Many's the time he's got me out of a bind that way. I run a mean hurdy-gurdy house, manage my girls, and charm the pants right off our customers, but when it comes to figuring, I'm useless. Ben has taken care of it for me for years. Before that, I like to went broke. You could do worse than have him as a full partner in Fallon Enterprises."

Rose hesitated and pinned Dessa with a flat stare.

"What does he think about you having all that money? Some men are funny in that respect."

"It doesn't seem to bother him. He says he really doesn't care if he has money, but if I'm set on keeping mine and earning more, he'll be happy to help me do so. What's important, Ben says, is what we are to each other. Having someone to love who loves you back." Dessa smiled. "I guess it is that simple, when you think about it. And the Lord knows I do love him."

Rose nodded and studied Dessa fondly. This child would be good for Ben. She had done a lot of growing up, and she cared about things most women didn't take the time for. Rose wondered idly if they had laid together yet. She would guess they had, the way they looked at each other, touched each other, exchanged secret smiles when they thought no one was looking.

Dessa took up her knife and began drawing lines on the tablecloth. After a while, she looked up. "Rose, do you think I should forget about Celia Cross? About my brother?"

"Lands, child. How would I know? If it's going to pester you to leave it be, then you'd best look further into it. I wish I could help you there, but I just can't recall knowing a woman by that name at all. Surely if she's from these parts, I'd a heard of her. Who else have you asked?"

"Ben asked around, he said. I'm not sure where. He told me to wait until he comes back and then we'll ride out to Alder Gulch and see if we can find Mitchell."

"Oh, my dear goodness, child. Don't the two of you go riding out into that outlaw country. All you'll do is get yourselves shot, or worse. Have you talked to Walter?"

"Ben did. He doesn't know anything, either. I don't know what to do next, Rose. I can't just let it be."

The two women left the restaurant together, but parted outside.

"Promise me you won't do anything crazy, you and Ben," Rose admonished. 'Talk to Walter. Maybe he'll get up a posse and go with you."

Dessa nodded, but she knew the futility of such a plan. Walter Moohn had no intention of riding into Alder Gulch, even if he could get some men to go with him. It was a foolhardy thing to do, and he had told Ben as much. If she and Ben did this thing, they would be completely on their own.

The woman showed up late that afternoon, when Dessa was actually watching for Ben and Wiley to return from their run to Three Forks.

Dessa had just lifted the curtain to study the street, then dropped it for at least the tenth time when she heard a light tapping on the back window. She was startled to see the dark, round face of an Indian woman peering in at her between cupped palms.

Quickly she crossed the room and raised the window.

"You must come with me," the woman said, her tongue and lips forming the words as if they were a foreign language.

She was dressed in buckskin that was quite soiled, but her shiny black braids were interlaced with crisp red ribbons and her mahogany skin was clean. During her quick study of the visitor, Dessa remained mute.

"Hurry. I have brought horses." The woman gestured, and Dessa saw two spotted ponies with blankets where the saddles should be, reins hanging down on the ground.

"Are you Celia Cross?" she asked, but knew without waiting for the reply that she was.

How could she not go with this woman, despite what Ben

had said? She could lead her to Mitchell. Still, fear formed a lump in her chest. Suppose it was a trick?

When the woman only watched her closely, she said, "I don't know. Please, where is my brother? How is he? How do I know you come from him?"

"Mitchell," the woman said. "He is my man and they will soon kill him. I cannot make him leave. He says that if that is to be, it will be, he will not run.

"But at night I hear them plotting, and each evening more of them sit on the opposite side of the fire, leaving Mitchell more and more alone. And it is as if he does not see, or perhaps he does not want to see.

"Please, you are his sister. He wishes to see you, and will not leave until he does. Come now."

Dessa's mouth went as dry as tinder. She thought of Mitchell, riding off to war, waving his hat above his head, back and forth, back and forth, until he rode out of sight shouting at the top of his lungs. How excited he was to be going off to fight for his country. And how she had cried for hours, for days. And she remembered all the years she'd thought him dead but sensed his spirit within her.

Seeing her hesitation, the Indian woman reached inside the bodice of her dress and pulled out a small deerskin bag. She shook two rings out in the flat palm of her hand.

Dessa gasped and took them. The smaller one, hers, with the Fallon markings surrounded by diamond chips, the larger one matching it.

Tears formed in her eyes. No one but Mitchell could have sent these rings, could have known what they would mean to her. It must be true, that he was an outlaw, connected to that dreadful Coody Land, else how had he come by her very own ring that Land had jerked from her finger, the ring that matched his?

"He watched you at the ceremony for the dead."

Dessa wiped her eyes and clutched both rings tightly. "The funeral for our parents? Oh, yes. I saw him. That was him. Oh, I knew. Oh, yes, yes. Oh, Mitchell. How is he? Is he well? What does he look like? Does he still wink and scratch at his ear when he teases? Oh, please, tell me."

Celia Cross nodded her head solemnly. "Come and you will see. Come before your man returns. There is great danger. Hurry, now." The Indian woman gave her the bag and Dessa dropped Mitchell's ring inside. The other she slipped on her finger.

She hesitated no longer. "Wait, wait right there. I'm coming."

Snatching at a wrap hanging on its hook, she pulled the door closed hurriedly without latching it and ran around the side of the house. Celia was astride her horse, holding out the reins of the other.

"White women do not ride with legs spread. Can you do so?"

Dessa nodded, and mounted the small Indian pony, clenching her knees tightly because there were no stirrups. She turned the horse to follow Celia Cross. They rode out across the hills, not keeping to the road, and at the rise, Dessa glanced once over her shoulder at the small town nested below. It looked very tiny.

Ben didn't bother to ask Wiley to slow at Dessa's; he simply hit the ground running, the Winchester gripped in one hand. He raced to her door and banged on it carelessly. It inched open under his fist.

He stuck his head in. "Dessa, honey. I'm back."

No reply. He called out again, then stepped inside. The small woodstove was crackling merrily, warding off the chill of the late fall day, but the back window stood wide open.

Ben muttered and went to close the thing. As he reached up for the sash, he saw two figures riding over the crest of the hill west of town. They were gone before he had time to study them much, but he could have sworn two women rode those spotted ponies, one an Indian.

Without thinking, he shouted Dessa's name, but the riders had passed out of sight beyond the ridge.

"Oh, dammit, Dessa." He knew immediately what had happened and he was furious. He'd told her not to go alone, and as soon as his back was turned, off she went.

Well, they weren't riding hell bent for leather. He'd catch them. He raced to the livery, saddled Beauty, and rose around the back of Dessa's house and up hill, the horse's pounding hooves kicking up mud. He was glad of the recent rains. There would be no trouble tracking the women if they got out of his sight. He halted his mount at the crest of the hill and gazed off into the distance for a moment. Ahead lay Alder Gulch, far off past what he could see. And below, threading their way through scrub and outcroppings of sandstone, were the women on the two spotted ponies.

Ben touched the scabbard that held his Winchester, then with grim determination dug in his heels. "Git. Git up." His voice sounded like sand gritting under bootheels.

The sun had set when the two women headed up the draw into Alder Gulch. Gold miners were gone now, the creek banks deserted. No rockers or pans, no bearded men squatting to grab at what color they could find. Prospectors had moved on to Wyoming, where the fever had caught new fire, giving this place back to nature. Here and there lay remnants of a deserted camp, a tin cup and plate, a broken-handled pick, a cross pounded into the earth marking the grave of someone who hadn't made it to the next strike.

Celia Cross hadn't spoken since leaving Virginia City. It was as if she had exhausted her entire knowledge of the white man's language persuading Dessa to make the journey. Dessa gave up asking questions when she heard no answers.

Several times they had stopped for water, letting the ponies wade out into the cold, clear creek to fill their own bellies, while they cupped up handfuls for themselves. Dessa thought of Ben, wondered what he would do when he returned to find her gone. He would be angry, perhaps even frightened. She should have left him a note or told someone, but there had been no time. She had been so afraid the Cross woman would grow impatient and ride away, and then she would never find Mitchell.

Then she thought of her brother. She had always been so proud when folks remarked how alike they were. How her dark hair and his curled just so away from the face. How their matching eyes would flame at precisely the same instant they got into some mischief. But Mitchell had always been smarter than her, braver, kinder. She couldn't picture him as an outlaw, no matter what the war had done to him. It just wasn't possible.

Her buttocks and thighs ached with the long ride, but still the Cross woman rode on, into the lengthening shadows. It was dark when they rounded yet one more outcropping on their steep climb up the mountain's face and spotted the campfires in a box canyon.

Celia Cross reined in her pony. "They have seen us. They know we are coming."

The words startled Dessa, for she had thought the woman would not speak again. "How can you tell?"

"Lookouts." She pointed high to either side of the trail.

"It's so dark, I don't see anything."

"They hear. They know."

"What will they do?"

"Nothing yet. I am Yank's woman, you are his sister. He still has his power. But I fear not for long. Come, we must go to him. He has waited so long."

"So have I," Dessa said. "Oh, Lord, so have I." Mitchell... Yank? Could it be?

As darkness slithered over the land, Ben began to curse softly. He couldn't track them at night, not until the moon came up, and it would be late this night, for the moon was on the wane. There was no doubt in his mind that they were headed for Alder Gulch, but that was a big place, and the outlaw camp wouldn't be easily found or easily approached.

He would get shot if he was spotted, and that would do Dessa no good at all. Of course, if her brother was really there, perhaps he could bluff his way in. Surely even an outlaw wouldn't want to kill the man his sister was going to marry, if Dessa had a chance to tell him.

At last, defeated by the dense night, Ben reined up and made camp. He'd had no time to pack food, but the bedroll was tied on his saddle, so he would have a place to lay his head and something to protect him from the cold that had descended quickly with the setting of the sun.

He fell asleep instantly, and didn't awaken until the moon crept past the mountain peaks to bathe him in its frigid light. Then he rose, repacked his horse, mounted up, and rode on. He didn't let himself think much about what might happen when he showed up in the heavily armed camp of these outlaws. He just kept thinking of Dessa, and how she turned her pretty head to study him when she was perplexed by his actions. And how it had felt to make love to her after Maggie was killed. That night he had experienced the pure sweet glory of life, and saw how it had to continue despite the agony of loss.

"Dessa," he whispered. He rode with his head bent down alongside the neck of the horse in order to follow the prints of the unshod ponies. "Dessa, my love. Don't go on without me. I'm coming."

The earlier brisk wind had calmed, and there was no answer in the hushed, moonlit night.

Ten

The camp was enormous, big as some of the settlements Dessa had seen along the railroad. Tents and primitive lean-tos were thrown up around a central gathering place. There a large campfire burned, and smaller fires flickered in front of some of the dwellings. In the flickering light, Dessa could make out men squatted around the fire, scattered groups of women and children, an occasional solitary figure off to himself. She could smell horses, knew by the sounds they made that they were kept nearby. The aroma of meat hung in the smoky air. The camp was very well hidden and would never be spotted by accident. Other than the posted lookouts, everyone seemed relaxed and unafraid. It was obvious they were quite sure no one would find them.

Guards such as those who had watched the two of them approach probably ringed the camp. There might even be no trail in except the way she and Celia had come, unless one were a mountain goat. Surely the outlaws had left themselves an escape route should they be surprised by a posse.

These observations came to a halt as she followed Celia's lead and dismounted. She looked all around, tried to spot Mitchell. Being so close to him gave her goose bumps, and she felt skittish, nervous, expectant, anxious. The moods came and went, nearly overpowering her in a turmoil of emotion.

"Where is he? Take me to him now," she finally demanded of the Indian woman.

Celia hailed a young boy who was running about with several other children, and he came to take the horses, staring at the ground after flicking a quick glance at Dessa.

"There are a lot of families up here," she said.

Celia didn't reply, but skirted the campfire. Everyone appeared to deliberately ignore their arrival, and Celia spoke to no one. She hurried on her way. Dessa had to run to keep up, and they approached a dirty white tent tucked back in the trees. It was obviously the largest and best of the dwellings. No others were nearby, though across the way were a variety of living quarters thrown up side by side. It would seem that her brother had drawn an invisible barrier around himself. A lamp burned inside the tent, and she could make out the shadow of a man.

Her heart pounded in her throat as Celia pulled the closed flap away and motioned her inside. The Indian woman did not enter with her, and when the flap closed at her back, Dessa finally let her gaze land on the face of the man standing before her.

Her brother's familiar high, wide cheekbones were stretched taut, eyes like nubs of glass reflected the lamplight, a scar through one eyebrow and up across his forehead led to a streak of white that spilled into locks of thick dark hair. The man at her parents' funeral. She had known all along, hadn't she? Deep down inside in that place that kept her brother's spirit alive, she had known it was him, and had been afraid to think it or speak of it.

He studied her intently before the somber expression fell away to be replaced by delight. "Dessa? My God, it is you. Oh, sweetheart. What a beautiful woman you've become." He spread his arms.

She cried out, unable even to utter his name as she flew into his waiting embrace. He held his long, lank body rigid, skin and muscle stretched like rawhide over bone, but he hugged her so tightly she could scarcely breathe. He smelled of whiskey and tobacco and leather and of being out in the cold too long.

"Dear God, little one. I thought I'd never see you again."

The voice was Mitchell's, but with a bitter edge to it that even being with her didn't soften.

She began to cry, burying her nose in his shirt and sobbing as if her heart were breaking.

"Here, now. No sense in that. Don't cry, Dessie, my little Dessie."

But she couldn't stop. She cried for all the years she'd thought him dead. She cried that mother and father would never know this joy. She cried for what the war had done to him.

He patted her back awkwardly, but he didn't release her. Instead he patiently held her while she cried it out. There in the middle of an outlaw stronghold where he ruled over the roughest bunch of men to ever gather in one place, Mitchell Fallon, alias the feared outlaw Yank, held his baby sister in his arms with a loving tenderness no one who knew him could ever imagine. Most, even seeing his kindness with their own eyes, would later deny it. It was what he himself would demand of them.

After a long while, when she could cry no more, they sat on the canvas floor among tanned hides and stacks of wooden crates marked *U.S. ARMY*, and talked.

She brought him up to date on what had happened since their parents' death because that's what he insisted on; she had wanted only to talk about him.

Naturally, the matter of lawyer Cluney and Andrew's betrayal came up.

In telling him, she stopped in midsentence, eyes glowing. "Mitchell, you're alive. You can—"

He couldn't help laughing, interrupting her.

She joined him for a moment, then grew serious. "I mean, Daddy wanted you to have everything if you were alive. And now you are and so we can… oh, Mitchell, I gave that terrible Andrew half of our… of your inheritance. If only I'd known for sure. But he wouldn't even let me have any money. I had to do something. Now you can write to Cluney and tell him you're very much alive and intend to claim your inheritance. I won't have to go through all that trouble of getting a lawyer and straightening out the mess.

"Oh, how could Daddy have mistrusted me so much? I loved him so, and then to find out he didn't even believe I could handle things. To let that horrid Andrew and P. L. Cluney have control."

Mitchell patted her awkwardly. "He'd be proud if he could see you now. I know I am. You've taken care of things very well. I see no reason for me to step in. I don't want Dad's money or his businesses. What would I do with them if I had them? I can't show my face in proper society, and I'll never be able to. Not in this country. Perhaps, though, I could do something… later to straighten it out… from a distance."

He studied the view through the open flap of the tent, not ready yet to reveal his plans. There was no point, for the chances he could pull off such a thing with his hide intact were not very good. No sense in getting her hopes up.

God, it was so good to see her this way, if only for a little while. The memory of this day would have to last him a lifetime, and he embraced her every word and expression.

"Ben says the railroads will go in soon up here," she said.

"Ben?" he asked, rubbing at the hair over one ear. "And

just who is this Ben?" Such banter seemed strange to Mitchell, having lived the life of the outlaw Yank for so long.

She tucked her head, feeling a bit shy talking about Ben Poole. It was hard to tell this man, whom she loved but no longer knew, about a personal part of her life that was still very new to her.

"He lives in Virginia City, and works for a freighting company, but he's so kind and gentle, and smart, too. He has one of those minds that latches on to figures and turns them inside out. It's amazing. He says we can go up north and put in some more stores, even thinks hotels might be a good idea. That is, he says, if that's what I want."

Mitchell listened intently, watching his sister's expressions with an unfamiliar longing. This was what he had sacrificed for his beliefs, this feeling of family and belonging, of sharing and love. Would he ever recapture that in his lifetime? He doubted it. The path he had chosen was a demanding and harsh one, and he feared he could never turn from it, would not be allowed to do so. Someone would always be just around the bend, waiting to remind him that he was an outlaw, a man wanted by every gunslinger and lawman in the territories. Even the Army would like to get their hands on the notorious Yank.

When Dessa finished telling him about Ben, he scratched at the hair above his ear and winked. "So my little one has found her a man to love? How is it with you and him?"

She felt for an instant as if she were twelve years old again and he was teasing her about an admirer in the schoolyard. 'You don't change, do you?"

"What?"

"That," she said, and reached over to tickle at the hair above his ear. 'You always did that when you were teasing me. That's how I knew when you weren't serious. And you still do it."

Mitchell's eyes glowed and he laughed deep in his throat, as if he weren't quite used to the experience. "I guess I did. And you didn't forget."

"I didn't forget anything."

"Remember where we hid our treasure?"

Dessa furrowed her brow, thinking back through the years. "The old—"

She held up a hand. "Don't tell me. I'll remember. Just a minute. I know, I know. In that old barn Daddy left standing when he tore down the cabin to build the new house."

Mitchell nodded.

"Under the feed trough. We pulled the boards loose and put them in there."

"I wonder if all those things are still there. The marbles and that round stone you found, the pink chert arrowhead we fought over. What are you going to do with the place, now that they're gone?" Mitchell asked.

Dessa covered her mouth with both hands. "Oh, heavens. I don't know. I guess I hadn't thought about it. With all the other things that have happened. That bastard Cluney trying to cheat me and Andrew helping him."

"Why, Sister. How you talk. Who taught you words like that? My sweet little girl, who talks with the mouth of a loose woman."

"I do not!"

"Did he teach you that, this Ben Poole?"

"No. Ben is the sweetest, kindest, gentlest man in he world. Oh, I don't know what I'll do with the place in town, sell it, I guess. But I think I'll keep the farm, Mitchell. So many memories. When I think of all of us together, it's always there where we were so happy, where we grew up and learned to embrace life. Oh, Mitchell."

He saw the pain in her eyes for all that was lost, and

practiced his laugh to turn her thoughts in another direction. "As you always did, you make me happy, Dessie."

"Oh, Mitchell. Why didn't you come back? We missed you so. It was so hard in Missouri, even after the war."

His eyes grew hard as flint. "You seem to have made it very well without me. The money just kept coming. Dad had a knack for making money, as I recall. I'm sure he profited well during the war."

Dessa snapped her head around to gaze at him. "Why, Mitchell."

He unfolded his long legs and rose, turning his back on her. "Don't tell me about hardship, Dessa. You had our parents, money, friends, all the clothes you needed, food enough. And nobody ever tried to take any of it away from you, even in the hardest times during the war and after."

She waited a long time before she answered the harsh words. Then she said, very softly, "They took you away from us, Mitchell. They took you and we never got over it, never."

He felt as if he had been struck in the heart with a lance. The forlorn words from his sister found their way into his soul as no others could have, and the pain grew until he feared he might burst out crying. After a few deep breaths he regained a bit of control, but still couldn't turn to face her once again.

She watched the rise and fall of his shoulders as he breathed, and wanted to reach out and touch him. After a while she did, and he shuddered, turned, and took her into his arms, burying his face in her hair.

Ben spotted the lookout, who made the mistake of rising for a brief instant, so that he made a silhouette against the moonlit sky. Ben had dismounted and left the black tied in a dense copse of trees half a mile or so back down the trail. In the war he had learned patience and fortitude when it came to sneaking up on the enemy or staying out of sight.

He now had to do both, and he took his time. Getting caught would do Dessa no good at all. One misstep, the cracking of a twig or the rattle of rocks, would betray him. He wasn't sure he could explain why he didn't ride into the place and trust Dessa's mysterious brother to save his bacon. Something didn't feel right to him. The entire situation was unknown, and Ben thought it best if he just snuck in for a look first.

By dawn he had worked his way near enough to the camp to smell smoke of the campfire and tobacco, the waste of humans and animals, to hear the cry of a baby, the snore of someone sleeping, the muted enjoyment of a man and woman making love.

As the sun lightened the mountainside, he had his first glimpse of the hideaway. People lived here, not monsters. Whatever they did, most of them did it out of necessity, in order to survive. They might kill him for that reason, too, and without any hesitation, if he wasn't very careful.

He watched the place come to life. A fat Mexican woman stirred up the central fire and began to pat out cornmeal between her palms, lying the flat cakes on a rock in the coals. A gray-haired white woman approached with a coffeepot and shoved it into the glowing embers. The two spoke softly for a few moments, then the older woman went back to the lean-to built from tree limbs and woven grasses. A couple of boys—one looked Indian—chased each other across the clearing, laughing.

It was hard to realize that this wasn't a town, just like any other town in the territory, but was instead the lair of one of the most hunted outlaws since the end of the war. Ben felt a tremor of excitement. He might soon come face-to-face with the notorious Yank, who had a bounty of $1,000 in gold on his head. A bounty he had no intentions of collecting.

A woman came from the dirty white tent across the way, stooping at first, so that he couldn't see her face. But he recognized Dessa just the same, and it was all he could do to keep from shouting at her. Another woman, an Indian, followed her out, and to-gether they walked around to the back and disappeared into the woods. While Ben was trying to decide if he should work his way along the periphery and try to catch up with the women, a tall, lean man stepped out and stretched his arms above his head.

"My God," Ben whispered, for he knew immediately who the man was. There was no mistaking the resemblance. This was Dessa's brother, no doubt about it. Same hair, same bone structure, and take away what harsh living had done, there was the same look about the eyes and mouth. From that white stripe in his hair there was no doubt, either, that this was Yank. It was described on every wanted poster in the territory.

Ben moved closer, and contemplated simply standing up and approaching the man to introduce himself. He halted when a rough-looking fellow meandered into his field of vision and began to talk to Yank.

"Make up your mind about the bank?"

Yank shook his head.

"Some of the boys ain't gonna wait no longer. Hell, it's ripe for hitting. What's wrong with you? Going soft in your old age?"

With mouth agape, Ben listened to the men actually discussing a bank robbery.

Yank finally spoke, a cutting edge to his deep voice. "We go when I say, we do what I say. I hear any more of this, you and your damned friends'll find yourselves at the bottom of the gorge. I'd been handling things a long time when you come here, and I'll be here when you're long gone."

"Maybe that's the problem. You been around too danged long for our taste."

Yank grabbed the man by the front of his shirt and lifted him up right into his own face. "Anytime, Grady. Anytime you please." He tossed the man backward as easily as if he weighed nothing.

Grady landed on his butt. He scrambled to his feet, and for an instant Ben expected him to tackle Yank, but instead he glared daggers at his leader, then walked away grumbling. He passed near Ben, so Ben heard the tail end of a threat. "... might be sooner'n you expect, Yank."

Sounded like there was trouble in outlaw land. So the warning from the Cross woman that Dessa's brother could be in danger hadn't been off target. But Ben couldn't be overly concerned about that. He was too worried about learning that Dessa and the outlaw Yank were brother and sister. He wasn't sure just what that might mean to their plans. She loved the brother she had lost, loved him dearly. Suppose she wanted to stay with him?

Immediately Ben dismissed that thought. Dessa would never do such a thing, he was just being foolish. His immediate concern had to be letting her know he was here, and the both of them getting the hell out with their hides in one piece.

Dessa watched her feet as she climbed up the rough incline behind Celia. What a way to live, especially for a woman, and more so if she had children. How did they do it, these women who loved men like her brother?

Off to one side she glimpsed deliberate movement and was astonished to see Ben peering from the woods and signaling to her. She cut her eyes toward Celia, who walked on around a curve in the path. Then she shooed Ben away with both hands. He shook his head and beckoned again.

Resigned, Dessa ran to him. "What are you doing here?"

"What are you doing here? I warned you not to come out here alone."

"My brother is here. Oh, Ben, Mitchell's alive and he's here. How could you expect me not to come?"

The expression of joy on her features was enough to make him forget his anger. "I just wanted to come with you, to keep you safe."

Dessa glanced nervously up the trail. "Well, you're here. Come on with me. We might as well tell Mitchell. I've told him all about you anyway."

He grabbed her arm, holding her back. "Did you know who he is?"

"What do you mean? Of course I know my own brother."

"No, I mean, did you know he's the outlaw Yank? The one the law's been chasing since the end of the war."

Dessa studied Ben hard. "No," she said firmly. "That's not true." She knew Ben was right, but couldn't help denying it aloud. No one need know, not even Ben. Perhaps saying it wasn't so would make it not so.

"Well, then, what do you suppose he's doing up here with all these thieves and cutthroats?"

"Hiding, that's all. He's in trouble and he's hiding."

"Oh, Dessa, think. He's in trouble, all right, not only with the law but with these men. They're fixing to mutiny. It wouldn't take much to set them all on him, and if they do that, they won't hesitate to get rid of you…me, too, for that matter. We've got to leave, now."

They both turned at the sound of footsteps shuffling through leaves up ahead.

It was Celia, coming back to see what was going on. "Dessa, where are you?"

Ben pulled at her arm. "Come on, come with me now!

"I won't, I won't." She jerked away and called out, "I'm coming, I'm here." She threw him one last dark look. "I won't leave my brother now that I've found him. Go on if you want. I'm staying."

Ben considered his options for only a moment. He could either cold cock her and drag her out of here or stay with her. He would not leave without her. As Dessa ran toward the sound of Celia's voice, he trotted along behind.

Ben's arrival in camp created quite an uproar. Upon learning that a man from the outside had actually penetrated the security of the camp, Grady, who was already at odds with Mitchell, called his followers together. He made no bones about his displeasure, and spoke so all could hear.

"He's old and soft, I tell ya. Living in the past when we could hit a stagecoach once a week and make out. Well, them days is gone. We either take what we want in some of these backwater towns or we figger a way to get on the trains.

"Them sons a bitches what ride them trains got more'n God, and they can share some of it."

A few nodded and cried out their agreement.

A red-haired, sunburned man shouted at the grumbling cluster of men around Grady. "Don't be fools. They could shoot ever man-jack of us, pick us off from them cars 'fore we could even get on board. I'm with Yank. He's done us good all these years."

Someone else spoke up. "Yeah, look what hurrahing Virginia City got Coody. Got him and the kid hung, that's what."

"Coody was a jackass, never had enough sense to come in out of the rain," Grady said. "He didn't have brains to pour piss out of a boot. But if we keep doing it Yank's way, we'll all starve. Women and kids and all. Winter's a comin'. What we supposed to do?" He scarcely took a breath before going on.

"And what I'd like to know is how'd this yahoo sneak up on us? First Yank's woman goes out and brings in an outsider, then this here other'n shows up. Next it'll be the posse, watch and see if it ain't."

During the squabble between the two sides, Yank remained aloof, his green eyes following the action with a bright glitter.

Dessa and Ben tried to remain in the background. She was feeling more and more uneasy about being there, even with Mitchell so close by. He had urged Ben to leave his Winchester inside the tent after Dessa introduced the two, claiming it might stir up even more trouble if Ben were armed.

Celia begged Dessa to talk to Yank. "I've been trying to get him to leave this place," the Indian woman said. "I'm afraid he'll stay until they kill him. His time has come and gone. Most of the men who came here with him are gone on, either dead or rode back to their homes to take up their lives once again. Perhaps he will do that, if you persuade him."

Dessa was amazed at the woman's vocabulary, and wondered what tribe she was from. Not that it mattered, but she had always thought of Indians as naked wild savages who grunted and scalped people. She had no idea they wore clothing and spoke English so well. The woman's suggestion seemed a reasonable one, so when things had quieted down a bit and everyone had gone off to eat their noon meal, Dessa approached her brother.

Mitchell sat on the floor of the tent, cleaning a long-barreled rifle. Despite a cold wet wind that had blown up by midmorning, Ben refused to come in, but remained squatted outside the door, on watch.

"I've been wondering, Mitchell, if you wouldn't like to go back to the home place, take care of it. I would like that better than renting it to strangers. Ben and I want to stay in Montana, or go on farther west."

"Can't do that," Mitchell said, and pulled a wad of cotton cloth attached to a string from the gun barrel.

"I don't understand."

"I'd be arrested before I could unsaddle my horse."

"What for? What have you done that's so terrible?"

He dropped the weight into the barrel once again, then glanced up at her. "Broke the law. I broke a lot of laws for a lot of years, and they'd like to string me up if they could just lay hands on me."

She swallowed over a hard knot in her throat. "Did you ever kill anybody?"

He continued to gaze at her, then busied himself once again with the cleaning chore. "Men in war kill people. That's the idea."

"I didn't mean then. I meant after."

Mitchell chuckled harshly. "What the hell difference does it make? Killing is killing, any way you look at it. They taught me how. What made 'em think I could just stop when they said it was over?"

"Oh, Mitchell." Tears filled her eyes. She thought of what killing had done to Ben. She couldn't bear the thought that her brother was a killer. And it was different, the war. Ben had said so, and she believed him.

"Well, what will you do now?" she asked when he didn't say any more.

He shrugged, and began to shove long gleaming brass cartridges into the breech of the rifle. The oily snick, snick as the ammunition slipped into place sent shivers running down her spine. Unconsciously she counted them. Sixteen. He could kill sixteen men with that horrid gun without ever reloading!

Frustration made her angry. "Mitchell, they'll kill you. I heard them talking. They're just a breath away from declaring war on you. And if they're as terrible as that awful Coody Land was, they won't care what they do."

Mitchell lay the Army-issue Henry rifle close by and drew his legs up, wrapping his long arms around them. "When he brought that ring in here, I almost killed him," he said, the bitter flavor back in his voice. "I thought he'd hurt you. I couldn't believe my eyes, couldn't figure out what in the world you were doing here. I knew it couldn't be by chance. Something had brought you here."

"As it turned out, it was you who brought me here."

He nodded solemnly. "I know, I found out. Celia admitted she wrote to them about me. That's when I first realized that she really loved me, that she didn't just latch on to me like the others, for the thrill of it. So I sent her to town. She found out about the fire and your arrival and the funeral." He smiled remotely. "I wanted to come right up to you, stand beside you out there in Boot Hill at their grave, but that damn sheriff was always right there, hanging on to you. I was afraid he'd guess who I was. Aw, hell, I was just too jumpy to be around the law at all. He probably wouldn't have known me, I had kept my hat on. I don't reckon there's a likeness anywhere, not even on the wanted posters, except for telling about this blamed stripe."

Celia entered, eyes wide. Right behind her, Ben stuck his head in the doorway. "Better git out here, trouble's a-coming."

Yank came to his feet, the gun in one fist like a growth that belonged there. "Fetch Poole's Winchester," he told Dessa curtly, and stepped outside.

Celia threw Dessa a frightened look and followed her man, leaving Dessa to get Ben's rifle.

Muted shouts and the drum of hoofbeats heralded the arrival of a frantic rider. He slid from his horse, panted out his message. "Posse's a-coming. Passed the word from down the line. Said ten, maybe fifteen men. Got a Indian tracker with 'em. Trackin' someone."

Grady roared and with one hand pointed his rifle in the direction of Yank, Ben, Celia, and Dessa. "You led 'em in. His woman led 'em here. What'd I tell you? What'd I say?"

He whirled around, facing the men. "Time we settled this. Who's ever with me, say so now. Rest of ya, look out 'cause we're gonna take care of the enemy in here first, afore them sons a bitches ride in."

Eleven

A shot rang out, fired from within the ranks of the traitors, and Grady spun around with a yell. Momentarily, the two factions ignored Yank to fire at each other.

Dessa broke into a run back toward the tent, shouting for her brother, then for Ben.

Ben grabbed her, rolled them both behind a fallen tree nearby. Celia followed. Mitchell stood out in the open, rifle to his shoulder, pulling off several shots from the powerful gun.

"Mitchell, for God's sake," Ben shouted. "Let's get the women out of here."

A bullet whined, chipping wood from the huge log behind which they hid.

'Yank, you bastard, I'll get you," Grady cried.

Whirling, Mitchell fired again in the direction of the shout.

He hustled to join the others. "Celia, take 'em to the cave. I got horses waiting on the other side, enough for the three of you. Git on 'em and ride, and don't look back."

Both Celia and Dessa cried out at once.

"I'm not leaving without you," Celia said firmly.

"Nor I," Dessa declared, watching Ben through slitted eyes.

"You have to understand," Yank said. "It's the war. It never ends. Always someone coming after you. I don't reckon the killing will ever stop."

Dessa grabbed his arm, tugged at him. Fear roiled deep in the pit of her stomach. 'You can stop it, Mitchell. Just say enough. Come with us. Now!"

Mitchell snorted. "Run away? Put down this gun and walk off? I don't know that I can. It always follows me."

Ben dragged Dessa away from the hold she had on her brother's arm. When he spoke, it was to Mitchell. "We've got to get the women out of here. Fight your damn war some other time. I won't get Dessa killed."

The battle that had raged in the center of the camp escalated as the posse rode in and joined it. For a while it appeared that everyone was shooting at everyone. Ben spotted the sheriff, saw an outlaw's rifle pointed at him, and without hesitation raised the Winchester to his shoulder, took aim, and brought down the man before he could shoot Walter Moohn.

Quickly he swiveled toward the woman, ducking his head. No time to think. No time. "You two go on, now, get started. I'll stay with Mitchell. We'll cover you and follow. Now, git, or I'll drag you both off and leave Mitchell to see to himself."

"I'm not—" Dessa began, but Ben pulled her to him.

"Go with her. I swear to you, if you don't, I'm taking you out of here. You know I can do it. Dessa, I love you. I won't see you hurt." He kissed her hard, then pushed her away. "Nor your brother. I'll stay with him."

Mitchell grabbed Celia's arm as bullets whined over their heads. "Take her to safety, and yourself, too. I'll be right there, I promise I will. Now go, dammit."

"You'll come?" Celia pleaded.

Hand over her mouth-to capture the kiss Ben had given her, Dessa watched her brother's brisk nod. Debris spat up around them in the hail of bullets.

"If you two don't get out of here, they'll kill us all," Mitchell shouted, and vaulted over the fallen log to take cover behind a tree. He raised the Henry and laid down a barrage of bullets. Ben joined in with the Winchester.

Celia dragged Dessa to her feet and, hunkered low to the ground, the two women clambered into the woods, leaving behind the sounds of battle.

Tears flowed freely down Dessa's cheeks and she sobbed so hard she could hardly stay on her feet. Ben. Oh, Ben. And Mitchell. God protect them, don't let them die. She couldn't bear to lose them.

Celia led her down the steep embankment, both women slipping and sliding, scarcely able to keep their feet under them. Beneath a bluff overhang she shoved Dessa into a dark cave like opening.

Battle sounds echoed in the distance, and they stopped to get their breath. No one appeared to have followed.

"Everyone knows about this. It's our escape in case we were ambushed... if anyone ever found their way up here and the men couldn't stop them. So we'll have to hurry. Some of the others will surely decide to run away, too."

"All the women and children. What will they do?" Dessa asked between gasps.

Celia was awfully quiet for a moment. "Who knows? Some will die, I suppose, others will live. They knew that before they came here."

"But not the little ones. They didn't know. How could he do this? How could he?"

"He did nothing; they did. Come on," Celia urged. "Time

to get moving. Follow me. Keep low, it is very close and we will have to crawl."

As they moved deeper into the cave, absolute darkness closed around them, so black they could only sense each other's presence by the sound of their breathing. Then they were crawling, feeling along the smoothly worn rock floor, shoulders rubbing the sides.

After what seemed like an eternity, a time in which all sounds of battle faded, a light appeared ahead, only a pinpoint, toward which they crawled on and on. Time held no meaning, nor did the terror that spurred them both. It was as if they had escaped into another world.

At last they reached the opening and Celia scrabbled out and to her feet, turning back to help Dessa.

"Will they come? Do you think they're okay?" Dessa asked.

"They will come," Celia said. "I'll find the ponies."

Shivering and hugging herself against the lash of a cold, wet wind, Dessa waited miserably until Celia appeared with three saddled horses.

"He went out last night. This is what he must have been doing," the Indian woman said.

"Only three?"

"Your man had not made his presence known."

Or her brother had no intention of getting out alive. Dessa pushed away the awful prediction and nodded, turned to stare at the black yawning hole from which they had emerged.

"He knew what would happen. We are to escape. It was his plan, you see." Celia sounded proud of her man, aloof from Dessa's concerns. "It will be all right, you will see."

Dessa shuddered violently with the cold. Dampness dripped from her hair, the air wet as rain. The Indian woman led the horses to the lee side of a huge boulder and signaled

Dessa to follow. There they hunkered and waited, unable to do anything else but hope and pray.

It was a long, frightening time before they heard the clatter of rocks coming from within the mountain. Ben emerged from the opening first and Dessa launched herself into his arms.

"Where's Mitchell?"

"Coming," Ben said, and held her close. The heat of his exertion warmed her shivering cold body.

Then Mitchell emerged from the dark hole in the mountain. Celia welcomed him in much the same way Dessa had welcomed Ben. All four huddled close.

Mitchell spoke with chattering teeth. "The sheriff and his men won out. We guessed it best to take off before he saw this damned white streak in my hair and put me in with the rest. Let's mount up and put some miles behind us before anyone misses us."

On the far side of the rocks, the horses waited, haunches turned to the wind. "Sorry there's not one for you, Poole," Mitchell said. "You and Dessa will have to double up. I didn't know you were coming."

"That's where you went last night," Celia said.

Mitchell nodded. "We'd better quit jawing and mount up. One or two of them gets away from the posse, they'll figure out pretty quick where we went, or hell, they're liable to tell the sheriff just for spite. Grady's bunch would like to see me strung up. Some are apt to be on their way already."

"What about the women and their children?" Dessa asked, reaching a hand up to let Ben pull her on the horse behind him.

"Sheriff had them all corralled in the big tent. Hollering and screeching, but I don't think any were harmed too bad. Some of the men didn't fare so well, though. Someone saw fit to shoot that bastard Grady." Mounted on an Appaloosa, Mitchell took off at a gallop, leaving the others to follow along.

At the mouth of the canyon, where the trail forked back toward town to the southeast or northwest into the mountains, he reined up.

"I don't know about you two, but me and Celia are going north, maybe all the way to Canada."

Dessa's heart skipped, then thundered in her ears. "But we just found you."

Mitchell rode close and reached out a hand to her. "I know, and I'm sorry, but I can't stay here. Everyone in the territories and back in the States would like to collect the bounty on my head. Some'd prefer to carry in this striped scalp. I'm tired of running, of looking back. I want some peace." He gazed with tenderness toward the Indian woman, watching and waiting patiently. "We want some peace."

"I can't let you go," Dessa sobbed, and clutched at his arm. "We'll go with you. Ben and I. We will, won't we, Ben?"

Ben watched in silence, his eyes like deep pools.

"And always be on the run?" Mitchell replied. "No. You stay. You and Ben help settle this territory. Use our father's money the best way you can. I'll see to that matter we spoke of. You'll hear from me."

"I've always been with you, little sister, and I always will be. Dear, sweet Dessie, go with Ben. Maybe we'll see each other sometime."

She shook her head back and forth. "No, oh, Mitchell, don't leave me again. I love you."

'Take her away, Poole, and you be good to her or I'll come back and find you."

Ben nodded grimly and shoved his heels in the horse's flanks. Dessa leaned her face against his back and clutched him around the waist, crying out her brother's name over and over. The heat of her tears soaked his shirt as he rode away without looking back.

Tired, wet, and cold, the couple rode into Virginia City, but didn't stop at Dessa's place or at the sheriff's office. They went directly to the Golden Sun Saloon.

Ben lifted his right leg over the saddle horn and jumped to the ground, then held up his arms to catch Dessa as she slid off.

"Go inside. Tell Rose and the rest what happened. If there are any men in there who can ride, send them out. Tell them to meet me down at the livery. I'll go round up some more men."

"Oh, no, Ben. What are you going to do?"

"Go help Moohn and his posse bring those outlaws in."

She clutched at his shirt front. "I won't let you go. What's the use? You said it was over. No, Ben, don't."

To watch him ride away was beyond anything she could imagine. All she wanted was for him to hold her close. Saying good-bye to Mitchell had been nearly more than she could bear. All she could think of was hanging on to this man she loved. Suppose he was killed out there. Then what would happen? What would she do? She couldn't lose him, too. It was irrational, she knew, but she couldn't help herself.

"It's all over, Dessa," he said softly. "Nothing will happen to me. Now you go on inside. Surely you understand that I have to do this, I have to see it through. For you, for Maggie, and for myself." Gently he pried her fingers loose and held both her hands in his, staring into her tearful eyes.

She nodded miserably. Of course she understood.

"Then hurry, do what I said. There's no time to waste."

She lifted her skirts, stumbled up onto the boardwalk and through the swinging doors, right into the arms of Rose Langue.

"What is it, child? What is it?"

As quickly as she could, Dessa related what was going on out at Alder Gulch. She left her brother out of the story completely. The moment she finished, Rose hurried to the bar. She pounded with a thick beer mug until she had everyone's attention.

"Walter Moohn needs help out at Alder Gulch. Every man-jack of you that can ride and shoot, get your tails out there, pronto. Ben Poole is waiting at the livery. Go, now," she shouted, and nearly every man bolted to his feet and ran out the door. They would rather face the guns of outlaws than the wrath of Rose Langue. Those few remaining either couldn't shoot, couldn't ride, or both.

Dessa collapsed in a chair at a table where Virgie and one of the girls sat nursing mugs of tea. Rose joined them and signaled Grisham, who brought over two more mugs of the steaming dark liquid.

"Now, child, tell us the rest. Did you find your brother? How did you escape that godawful nest of thieves? Wiley Moss saw Ben light out, and it didn't take long for the sheriff to figure out what was going on, with you missing, too."

Dessa told Rose about finding Mitchell only to lose him again, but she didn't reveal that he was the hunted outlaw Yank. She would never tell that to a living soul as long as she lived. She hoped that when this was all over, everyone could be made to believe Yank was dead, shot in the battle with the sheriff and his men. It was time Mitchell had a little peace, and Celia, too. She prayed they were safe, and that reminded her of the danger Ben would be riding into, so she added a prayer for him, too.

Even riding hard as they dared, it took Ben and his makeshift posse some time to reach the place where the night before he had tied Baron in order to sneak up on the outlaws' fort. He reined up and let the clatter of their arrival die away. In the silence, they should have been able to hear gunfire if the battle had broken out again. It had been all but over when he and Mitchell had left—the man would have it no other way—but something could have happened to turn the tide, and he hadn't wanted to chance such a thing.

Baron raised his head from nibbling at a patch of grass and whickered at their arrival, but that was the only sound they heard in the somber air that spat flecks of wet snow into their upraised faces. Ash-gray clouds hid the mountain peaks and darkened the afternoon sky. In the thick air hung the smell of gunpowder and campfire smoke.

Good God, suppose they were all dead.

"Come on, men," Ben shouted. "This ain't no time to be shy. Let's get up there."

Throwing caution to the wind, he headed the sorrel Yank had supplied up the narrow winding trail, trusting the dozen or so men who had come with him to follow. Before they had gone more than a few hundred feet, they heard the thud of hoofbeats, the low grumble of voices, a nervous ripple of laughter.

Ben raised a hand. "Hold up, there. Sheriff... Sheriff Moohn, that you?" He waited, wondering what he would do if he was leading the men into the face of the outlaws. But he didn't think so. He figured if any of the outlaws had survived the battle, they would ride out hell-bent for leather. This had to be the sheriff and his men.

A horse and rider came in sight from around a sharp bend in the trail. "Who the hell is that? Say, or I'll shoot!"

"It's me, Ben Poole. Same to you up yonder. Identify yourself."

"It's Wiley Moss. The sheriff took a bullet, but he's okay. We got the sonsabitches, Poole. You hear me, we got 'em, ever one."

Almost everyone, Ben thought with a small grin.

The undaunted Wiley kept up his chatter as the two bands of men joined forces to herd the captured outlaws toward Virginia City. "It's gonna take a while to sort things out, and we'll have some burying to do. They's sure a bunch of caterwauling females and young'uns to deal with come morning, but they're okay.

"We thought it best to git this bunch in to the jail and the sheriff to the doc first off."

Ben nodded and rode along beside his friend, his mind back at the Golden Sun Saloon with Dessa.

Dusk had a firm grip on the land by the time the weary riders plodded back into Virginia. Ben led the black gelding, and left him and Yank's sorrel at the livery. Wearily he trudged to the Golden Sun and joined the merrymakers. The saloon's walls were bulging and Grisham, Rose, and two of the girls busily drew beer for everyone.

"On the house," Rose shouted to a tumultuous uproar.

The men were high-strung and boisterous, talking too loud, laughing too hard, drinking too much. Ben had seen it before, this emotional outburst after a victory. All he wanted was to go somewhere quiet and be with Dessa, hold her close, celebrate their survival. One look at her told him she felt the same, and he drew her through the celebrating crowd to a table in the far corner of the saloon.

Moohn lay upstairs, where the doctor was busy cleaning his wound. The bullet had passed through the fleshy part of his shoulder, and it wasn't long before the sheriff staggered downstairs, a white bandage wrapped around his arm where the shirtsleeve had been ripped away.

"Walter Moohn, you ought to be in bed," Rose scolded, and wiped her hands to go to him. Together they settled at a table.

Dessa and Ben sat close together, tentatively touching as if to convince themselves they were both alive and unhurt.

"Will you marry me now, Dessa?"

She cupped his cheek in her palm. She already missed Mitchell, but just knowing he was alive made the ache in her heart less painful. Besides, there was this wonderful man, holding her, loving her.

She looked deep into his clear blue eyes. "Oh, yes, Ben. Now, this minute, if you say so. I was so afraid for you."

"It's okay. Everything's okay now. It's as if all this made me into a different man."

She laughed and leaned against him. "Not too different, I hope. I kind of like you the way you were, if you know what I mean." She lay a hand high on his thigh suggestively.

"Dessa, shame on you," he said. "Oh, God, it feels good to be with you like this and know it's forever. Just think of what we're going to do together. It's all out there waiting for us, and I can't wait to get started." At last he truly belonged to someone who loved him. He could put all the memories to rest, once and for all.

"Do you suppose we could get married now, this very minute?" she asked. "The way I'm feeling, I don't want to sleep alone tonight."

He held her back a ways so he could study her lovely face framed by long strands of flyaway hair. Then he laughed and hugged her up close. "Let's just go find the preacher."

Together they rose and slipped quietly through the swinging doors, leaving the victory celebration behind. The big Montana sky deepened to velvet sprayed with the glitter of millions of stars. Clouds that earlier had dropped snow glowed like gunmetal on the horizon to the southeast and there was a bite in the air.

Ben gazed down into her eyes, his own gleaming with love.

"Want me to carry you?" he whispered.

She remembered the night he had come to her out of the dark, his strong arms sweeping her up as she collapsed, and she smiled.

"Yes, that would be wonderful."

He laughed, swung her easily off her feet, and carried her down the center of the deserted street toward the church.

Velda Brotherton writes from her home perched on the side of a mountain against the Ozark National Forest. Branded as *Sexy, Dark and Gritty*, her work embraces the lives of gutsy women and heroes who are strong enough to deserve them. After a stint writing for a New York publisher, she has settled comfortably in with small publishers to produce novels in several genres.

Facebook: Author Velda Brotherton
Twitter: @veldabrotherton
www.veldabrotherton.com